The Heart of a Gangsta 2

Jerry Jackson

**Lock Down Publications and Ca$h
Presents
The Heart of a Gangsta 2**
A Novel by *Jerry Jackson*

The Heart of a Gangsta 2

Lock Down Publications

P.O. Box 870494

Mesquite, Tx 75187

First Edition December 2017

Printed in the United States of America

Lock Down Publications
Like our page on Facebook: Lock Down Publications @
www.facebook.com/lockdownpublications.ldp
Cover design and layout by: **Dynasty Cover Me**
Book interior design by: **Shawn Walker**
Edited by: **Lauren Burton**

Jerry Jackson

Stay Connected with Us!

Text **LOCKDOWN** to 22828 to stay up-to-date with new releases, sneak peaks, contests and more…

Thank you!

Submission Guideline.

Submit the first three chapters of your completed manuscript to ldpsubmissions@gmail.com, subject line: Your book's title. The manuscript must be in a .doc file and sent as an attachment. Document should be in Times New Roman, double spaced and in size 12 font. Also, provide your synopsis and full contact information. If sending multiple submissions, they must each be in a separate email.

Have a story but no way to send it electronically? You can still submit to LDP/Ca$h Presents. Send in the first three chapters, written or typed, of your completed manuscript to:

LDP: Submissions Dept
Po Box 870494
Mesquite, Tx 75187

DO NOT send original manuscript. Must be a duplicate.

Provide your synopsis and a cover letter containing your full contact information.

Thanks for considering LDP and Ca$h Presents.

Jerry Jackson

Chapter One

Icey held the phone up, staring at the man she loved with fear. How long had he been standing there? What had he heard thus far? And why was he standing there holding a gun? He was looking at her with an expression she'd never seen before.

Pimp was a serial killer. He was unlike any man she'd ever met. He was like one of those guys people read about in the newspaper or saw on the news channel making history. She didn't ever think she'd meet a guy like him in person, let alone fall in love with one.

People were fooled by his youthful look and humble approach. He carried himself well, with respect, and his grace was charming to its max.

How could she not see? Brad was right all along, but she was blinded by Pimp's good game and sexy features. Icey had held so much faith, so much hope every day with them together. It felt so good.

Icey looked up from the gun in his hands. She looked him in the eyes with her own, pleading for her life, praying he had time to understand before he acted. She spoke into the phone after a moment.

"Ma, I'll call you right back." She had to cut the conversation short. Without giving her a chance to reply, Icey hung up the phone. She walked around her desk, heart beating wildly in her chest.

"Answer me, Icey," Pimp said. He closed the door behind him, gun still in hand.

Icey swallowed hard. She did not want to say the wrong thing. She had to tell the truth, but the truth would probably get her killed.

Pimp didn't trust her. She didn't blame him, either,

because if the shoe was on the other foot, if he had a federal best friend and his home was bugged, then she would feel how he must feel.

Icey reached out toward Pimp, but failed to touch him when he pulled away.

"Answer me," he said in a vicious voice.

Icey knew it was now or never. She knew her time had run out.

"I found your hidden room. I know the truth now. I'm hurt, I'm confused, I'm scared, and I don't know what to do. I love you, and I don't wanna see you hurt. I covered everything up before I left 'cause you said the feds were coming. But if I found it, then don't you think the feds will, too? What are you going to do now? Especially if that room is found?" Icey said everything out of fear and concern.

Pimp walked away. He had a thoughtful look on his face as he tucked the gun in his waistband.

Inside her office was a painting Icey had been working on. It was a picture of them both in an embrace that was nearly finished.

Icey's heart beat wildly as she contemplated her next move. Pimp's back was to her. She could run, if she wanted. Run and scream for her life. *But was it that serious?*

He had a gun. His facial expression was unlike one she'd seen. So, yes, it was serious.

Should I try to hit him? Could I knock him out with something? It wouldn't work. It couldn't work, she thought as she pocketed her phone.

Love and faith made her stay and wait for his reply. Fear held her captive, but love also kept her there. She was pregnant with his child. *Pimp wouldn't hurt me. Or would he?* was her next thought.

He finally turned around to face her. He stood in place while she did the same. Pimp was about to open his mouth to speak, but stopped. He looked up to the ceiling for a moment's time with a shake of his head, then back down to the woman who carried his child.

"Icey, right now my mind-state isn't at its best. My trust is empty and unmotivated toward you and everyone involved." Pimp began to walk toward her. "Lemme tell you something. When I fell in love with you and found out about ya boy, Brad, I made up in my mind that if you was the reason I failed, I love you so much I was willing to take that chance. But now I'm not feeling that way anymore. See, baby girl, what you didn't know was I also made a promise years ago to myself to not let nothing or no one stop my mission. My father is most important to me, Icey. I'm just being honest. So the shit you found in that room? Yeah, that's the real me. That's my life, that's my mission."

Pimp stood face-to-face with her, neither one moving an inch. Icey's mind was in overtime processing all he said. Pimp's mind was battling with itself, confused about his next move.

"Baby." Icey reached out and took his hand. Pimp didn't pull away this time, just stood there looking deep into her eyes. Icey placed one of Pimp's hands on her stomach. Their eyes still locked, she said "Whether wrong or right, I'm committed to you. I don't like it, but I'm not going anywhere. I'll protect you, just protect us. I know it's hard to trust people, and even me because of the stuff that has happened, but you gotta believe me. I'm not against you, Savarous."

"I hope not, Icey," was all Pimp said.

He felt his phone vibrate a few times, so he pulled away from her to check his calls. Icey was feeling hopeful, but still scared because she knew what was in his house and prayed the feds didn't stumble across it. Because if so, then what?

"Savarous, what's the plan as of now? What do you want me to do?" Icey asked.

Pimp was sending someone a text message. He looked up from the phone screen. "Nothing for right now. Act normal and I'll meet you at the house later," Pimp shot back and started texting again.

"I thought the feds was at the –"

"They're gone now. We good there. I got something else I gotta go handle. I'll meet you later." Pimp pocketed his phone, tucked his gun, and left her office. When he walked out, she let out a breath of pent-up air. Her stomach was in knots and her hands were shaking badly. She was happy Pimp didn't hurt her, that he found some form of trust in her, and even gladder the feds didn't find anything in the house.

***

"Fuck! Fuck! Fuck!" Pimp screamed as he mashed the gas through traffic after leaving Icey. He was headed back to the airport, his mind racing more than a million miles per hour. He was trying hard to figure a way out of his fuck-up. Moving in and out of the Miami traffic, he took out his phone and called Shaw.

"Yo."

"Meet me in the Westend mall in two hours, urgent, no clothes, no nothing. I got all that," Pimp said and hung up the line, then called his lawyer back.

"Attorney Brown," the lawyer picked up his personal line.

"Did you see the tape yet?" Pimp had fucked up bad, and he knew it.

"Clear as day. Savarous, what was you thinking?" the lawyer asked.

"It wasn't me. I was in North Carolina. I got video proof, store receipts," Pimp lied and knew his lawyer would want to see. He already had his white college buddy working with two store managers on their way to the north. Pimp knew he only had four hours to make up for his fuck-up or he would go to war with every police force in the world before going to jail.

"This gonna be a very hard one, Savarous. Police all over are looking for you right now. If you have video proof, store receipts, then turn yourself in like the first time," his lawyer advised him.

"You want me to turn myself in?"

"Like, right now."

Pimp pulled up to the Miami airport run by an underground mafia dude he paid good money to. He climbed out, phone still glued to his ear.

"Ok, give me 'bout two hours and we'll meet in Atlanta so we can go together," Pimp told his lawyer, who agreed, and they both hung up the phone.

Pimp was met at the gate by two armed mafia men. They led him through toward an already-running G-4 jet. He quickly made his way onto the jet and found his seat.

Pimp had made the biggest mistake of his life by killing Diamond on video—a video he didn't realize was found or formed. He was moving too fast, moving without thinking. When he finally got her address, all Pimp wanted was her dead, so he made no plan, plotted no move, counted no steps. He just went in and murdered her and left as quickly as he came.

Now in Atlanta, his face was all on the news, radios were broadcasting the murder, and there was a manhunt nonstop. The video was proof Pimp was the killer.

Pimp was the kind of guy who kept everything under control at all times. He never let people see him sweat, but right then he was breaking. Right then he was in doubt 'cause time wasn't on his side.

The guy finally took off after twenty minutes of sitting – twenty minutes that pissed Pimp off 'cause he really didn't have the time. Life was moving extremely fast for him right now, and it seemed he was gullible to the pressure around him. He was really slipping on how he operated.

It took them forty-five minutes to land in North Carolina, and Pimp took another ten minutes to meet up with Randy and one of the Foot Action store managers outside of the store. Time was running out.

"What's up, bruh? You ready?"

They all shook hands.

"Yeah," Pimp replied. The manager walked into the back of the store while Randy and Pimp walked in and shopped, buying two pairs of shoes each. They made sure to be seen good by video. Both made it to the counter and posted up, talking and laughing while the clerk rang up their shoes.

After being sure they were caught on video, Pimp and Randy met up in the back with the manager, where Randy started doing his magic on the time and date of the tape. Pimp kept looking at the time 'cause it was moving too fast.

Every call or text to Pimp's phone was ignored until

Randy had his end of the deal going good. Once Randy had it hooked up, Pimp paid him twenty grand, and the manager the same amount.

Pimp and Randy went to another store a few blocks away. They repeated the same thing, and Pimp called and gave his lawyer the addresses where he could go pull the tapes and check the receipts.

"You should be in Atlanta now right?" Mr. Brown, his attorney, asked.

"Yeah, I'm waiting on you," lied Pimp.

"Okay, give me an hour and a meet spot," the lawyer told him.

Pimp agreed and hung up the phone, he rushed through traffic back to the plane, at the same time blowing Shaw's phone up with all kinds of messages from a burnout cell phone.

You killed my sister Shawn!!

That was Shaw's real name. Pimp text again.

You gonna die for that.

He tossed the phone on the seat to focus on the traffic until he made it to his flight to Atlanta. It didn't take him that long at all to get there. Pimp took everything he bought and climbed back on the mafia flight. He knew he had to be extra careful in Atlanta. He knew he couldn't be seen by anyone if he wanted his plan to go right, and he hoped Shaw made it over in time. Time was ticking, and for the second or third time in his life, Pimp was nervous.

***

He was posted up at one of the new trap houses on the west end, waiting on Shaw while texting with his lawyer back and forth.

Too much was going on at once. Too much had happened all out of nowhere. Pimp was getting sloppy, he thought. He had to be 'cause his face was all on the video, all over the news channels. "Stupid-ass bitch, Diamond," Pimp mumbled under his breath, knowing she was the reason behind all of this fuck-shit. All she had to do was abort the kid and keep her life. Now she had forced his hands, and again he must do something he really didn't want to do.

Pimp shook his head at thoughts of what had to take place in order for this to work. His heart pounded away in his chest. He didn't wanna do it, but he had no other choice.

When he met Shaw at the west end trap house, Pimp had cloths, guns, and a vest for him. He tossed them to Shaw when he jumped out of the whip.

A few dudes were in the yard fixing a bike while Donte sat on the porch, running his mouth on the phone. Pimp dapped him up as he walked into the house behind Shaw.

"Bruh, I been getting strange-ass messages to my phone. What's up, though? What's the plan?" Shaw turned around, holding up the vest. He knew Pimp kept something up his sleeve. It was about the money with Pimp and since they were young, Shaw would do anything for Pimp, without questions. But this time something just didn't feel right. This time Shaw didn't wanna get involved with whatever it was.

"I got this issue over here on the north side drive. We 'bout to pull up, take a check and some bricks, probably murk a few bitches. They know I'm coming, but don't know when. Shit just popped off not long ago," Pimp lied.

"And what's up with this shit you on the news for?"

Shaw wasn't convinced.

"That's nothing. I'm try'na go handle this money situation first, tighten up," Pimp waved it off, pulling his phone out. Shaw started to say something, but didn't. He got dressed in the gear Pimp had for him.

Since growing up together, both guys always held each other down. Pimp had trust in Shaw just like Shaw had trust in him. Cutthroat wasn't Pimp's way of life, but it was in him, and that was the same reason he aimed his gun at Shaw when he bent down to tie his boots.

Boom, boom.

Blood and brains came out of the front of Shaw's face as his body leaned over and hit the floor. The hollowtips tore up his face, killing him instantly.

Pimp heard commotion in the house, heard niggas running to the back where he and a dead Shaw were. The first person to burst through the door was Donte, followed by his crew.

"What's up, bruh? What da fuck?" Donte said once he saw Shaw laid out on the floor.

Pimp looked from the body up to Donte's eyes. "The nigga was stealing. Leave this shit just like this, get all the work and money, take it to Miami." Pimp paused and looked at Donte's crew. "Take these niggas, too. I'll be there in a few."

"Okay, y'all, wrap this shit up," Donte ordered his men. He then pulled Pimp to the side before he left. "Stealing, bro?"

"Fuck yeah, too much money," Pimp lied with a straight face and left to go meet up with his lawyer.

Jerry Jackson

Chapter Two

You Not From Miami, So Fuck You!

Champ was tired of laying low, running from a nigga everybody but him thought was God. Pimp had niggas shook 'cause he bodied two people in front of the whole hood. It didn't faze Champ or stop him from running up on one of Pimp's main spots in the projects: The Blue Store, owned by a two-faced, wannabe dreadhead.

Champ had not one problem running up, taking Queen off for his money, drugs, and life. He was only nineteen years of age and making a name for himself in the Miami streets. Champ already had enemies who wanted him dead, and he didn't give a fuck.

Champ was street from the hardest part of Miami, so he wasn't a push over. He mimicked his fear tactic from murder black and already was a fighter. Nobody dared try him.

Once he saw niggas feared him, he started taking money and beefing hard daily with any and everybody. It didn't matter.

He had three bricks and a hundred grand to split up with his two cousins. Word on the street was some of the pokey projects niggas was looking for Champ. No police were looking for him, meaning one thing: the beef would be handled in the streets.

Either way, Champ wasn't bothered by it at all. He picked up his gun and phone and dialed his cousins Tuck and Mel.

"I'm on the way over to the hood, fuck them pokey bean niggas. I'm not about to keep sitting in no MF house waiting like some bitch."

"Now, I'm feeling that same flow, cuz, but Mel is bugging. Said niggas said it's ten bands on each of our heads. Me, I'm like *fuck that shit*," Tuck shot back through the phone. He was the wildest out of the two brothers. He had big nuts and a lot of heart.

"What they made guns for, Tuck?" asked Champ.

"For us to kill a bitch," his cousin laughed through the phone.

"Exactly. So where's that nigga Mel, anyway, cuz?" Champ asked while strapping up to leave.

"That scaredy-ass nigga caked up with his BM in the room," Tuck replied.

"Okay, I'll be through in a minute, cuz-o."

Champ hung up the phone, he was already dressed down in all black, two guns, two extra clips. He was prepared for war tonight, if they must. Tonight he was gonna post up on the block, not giving two fucks what the outcome may be.

When Champ walked out of his bedroom, his girlfriend Gigi was braiding her daughter's hair. Gigi was older than him by five years. She was his ride-or-die, had been like that for three years, since they met.

"And where is you headed?" she asked once she saw him about to leave.

"To the block for a minute. Wassup?" Champ stopped before going out the door.

"Don't go out there on that stupid shit. Remember, you got life on the way, nigga," she patted her stomach.

"I'm good, ma, trust that. I'll fuck some shit up, but never get fucked," Champ boasted, something she was turned on by. His arrogance and confidence were so captivating.

Champ walked out of the crib, closing and locking

his door. He had been ducked off on the other side of town, away from Pine Street, and now it was time to pull up and show face, fuck the consequence.

Outside, Champ climbed into his girl's car. He pulled off down the street to a local park. Getting out of the car, he put some gloves on and pulled his hat low over his head. He made his way over to the park's bathroom. Inside, Champ found the stall he was looking for. It was there, in the roof, where he pulled the bag of money and dope out. Quickly, Champ made his way to the car, climbed in, and pulled off.

***

Champ met up with Tuck and Mel. They were posted up in a Honda Civic with heavy tints. They sat unnoticed, watching the block, looking for one dude in particular: Pimp.

Word hit the streets that Pimp was looking for them, so they decided to get him before he could strike on them.

"Man, that nigga not gonna pull up out here," Mel said while watching the block movement. He really didn't know Pimp, but nobody was that stupid to pull up on the block knowing the streets wanted your head.

"One thing about it, he couldn't hide forever," Champ said.

"Pull up at the blue store. Let's see the faces of who's out there," Tuck told Mel, who was driving, and of course Champ liked the idea.

"Hell yeah," spoke Champ, gripping his gun tight.

"Y'all niggas must be crazy. Didn't you hear me say niggas got a check on us? We don't know who the shooter is. Fuck all this shit y'all talking, we 'bout to go split that check and them bricks up. Y'all niggas on some crazy shit, for real," Mel crunk up.

"Man, you the crazy one," Tuck shot back. Mel was the one who thought he ran everything 'cause he was the oldest. Tuck didn't like that.

Mel pulled off in the Honda and went the opposite direction of the blue store.

"Man."

"Man, what?" Mel turned in his seat to face Champ in the back seat. "Wassup?"

"I'm just saying, I'd rather get this shit out the way, that's it, cuz."

"And I'm saying the same thing, but first thing first, we 'bout to split out."

"And then we coming back out?" Tuck asked.

"Yeah, I'm with that," Mel replied.

It wasn't thirty minutes later when they pulled up at Mel's auntie's house where the money and dope were stashed the second time by Champ earlier. The boys thought it would be a good idea to duck off at their aunt's house, being that nobody knew 'bout her.

All three boys got out of the Honda Civic. Mel noticed two surburbans parked in front of the house and wondered who it could be. People didn't just visit his aunt like that. She was a hidden-type person who stayed away from life. It wasn't the police because the two trucks had dopeboy rims on them.

He eased his gun out, and Tuck and Champ did the same. Mel crept up slowly to the door. The lights were on in the living room. Mel opened the door, and when he did he was shocked to see his aunt and her husband tied up, guns aimed at both of their heads.

"Might as well join the party, my friend." A big, black

dude sat in Mel's aunt's favorite chair, his legs crossed with a gun in his hand, looking unfazed, unbothered, and murderous.

***

Pimp was leaving the homicide unit with his lawyer. After hours of sitting through with the DEA and the detectives, the feds even came and questioned some of Pimp's whereabouts. His lawyers had everything air tight, leaving the feds and the state no other choice but to let him go.

"Savarous, I highly recommend that you chill and let most of what you're doing go. We're almost to the point where we can see some light on your father's case. Don't put yourself in beside him," one of his lawyers said at the airport.

Pimp was texting on his phone. He looked up and said, "You right, Jimmy. Thank you again," and with a pat on the shoulder from Pimp, he walked off and headed toward the G-4 flight. Pimp knew he was playing close to the fire. He knew he had to also make a decision whether he would deal with Icey or not. She had him confused to the point she didn't even look the same anymore.

Did he still love her? He couldn't even answer his own question. Pimp could not trust her anymore, or could he? Could he look at her the same? He would soon find out.

Back in Miami, everything was good. The FBI found nothing on him or his club, which meant business could go on as usual at least for Montay, 'cause Pimp had other plans.

Montay had been holding everything down for him.

Donte and his crew had made it to Miami also, so that was a plus. Pimp had a plan for the dudes who took Queen's life, but first things first, he had to figure out what he and Icey were gonna do.

Pimp finally made it to the airport. The landing was smooth, and that's what he paid good money for. Pimp walked down the ten steps to a golf cart, ready to take him to the front. Montay was picking him up.

When he made it to the front of the airport, he saw Montay's gray Escalade on nice rims, Montay stood out just like the dope boy he was, and neither guy cared. Pimp made his way over with nothing but his phone. He got into the truck, and so did Montay.

"What's up, nigga?"

"Shit, you tell me?" Pimp closed the door and Montay pulled off.

"I done had a few niggaas roughed up, got a few answers," Montay spoke.

"Like what?"

"Champ, some niggas name Mel and Tuck. All these niggas cousins or some shit. They been in hiding, which confirm they was the MF who hit us."

"Oh yeah?"

"Yeah. Like I said, I done had a few niggas flipped. I'm just glad you back, 'cause the block in demand, and niggas are talking crazy. I guess niggas thought you wasn't gonna beat the feds."

"I know, right?" replied Pimp, putting more plans into his thoughts, then he added, "So nobody came 'cross Champ, den?"

"Nobody," Montay answered.

Twenty minutes into the ride, they made it to Pimp's condo in downtown Miami, where Donte and his crew awaited him. Everyone was quiet when the two entered. Donte stood up.

"Wassup, big bro?" he asked Pimp after they pounded each other.

"It's a lot of fuck-shit going on, but we'll get down to the bottom of it. First things first, we gotta handle some beef, then we gon' continue to get this money," Pimp said and got approval nods from everyone.

"So, what's plan A?" asked Donte.

"First things first, I murdered Shaw 'cause he was stealing. I'm not playing with no nigga about my check. If y'all niggas want y'all check right, then don't play about mine's. I'm not none of you niggas' leaders, I'm just the nigga wit' the means. Tonight we gonna slide through and shake up these young niggas out here on Pine Street, then we pulling and posting the block. Show face and let these pussies in Miami know who run shit and who don't."

"I'm ready." One of Donte's guys rubbed both his palms together.

"Montay, c'mere, bruh," Pimp called Montay to one of the three rooms. Montay walked in behind Pimp, closing the door.

"What's good?"

"This the move." Pimp walked to the bed, and from under it pulled a bag. He tossed it on the bed, and inside were six kilos, all broken down in zips. "Seven-fifty a pop. We upgrading the business 'cause our stay isn't long here, my nigga. I got 'bout twelve mo' kilos, and we out," Pimp said.

"What about the club? That bitch making good paper," Montay wanted to know.

"You can push that bitch if you want when I dip, but I'm gone, my dude. I'll sign all paper to you, my nigga"

"Damn, nigga, these folks must got you shook?" Montay asked in a joking manner, but was serious.

"Nawl, bruh, I got big shit popping. Way bigger than Miami," Pimp replied and zipped the bag up. "We set up shop at the club tonight after the showdown. Take these to the spot and put heavy security around the blow until we can get to it. I'm 'bout to prep Donte and his folks on how we moving tonight. Me and you will link up so I can tell you what's what later tonight."

"Bet that," replied Montay and took the bag Pimp gave him. They both walked into the living room. Montay went out the door and Pimp took a seat on the sofa.

"Here's the plan."

Chapter Three

Shit Has Hit the Fan

"What the fuck!" Champ spoke. He knew not to try anything 'cause his aunt's life was on the line. He knew he was defeated because it was six niggas with choppas against three niggas with handguns. He could tell his aunt's husband had been roughed up by the noticeable marks on his face. His aunt's facial expression was of a woman who'd recently been crying; dry tears marked her face, now replaced with a mean mug.

Pimp had caught them bad. He had been one step ahead of them. Champ was heartbroken knowing they wouldn't get to enjoy the money and dope they hit for 'cause he saw the bag that held the stuff on the floor next to the big guy.

How did this nigga Pimp know where to find them? He was more plugged than the three boys thought, because he caught them slippin' with their pants around their ankles.

"Drop them guns while y'all at it, and step on in."

Champ, Mel, and Tuck all were stuck and didn't know what to do, what to say, or how to react. Mel notice he had a mouthful of gold teeth with long dreads.

Two of his men disarmed the three boys, leaving them standing there at the mercy of Big Guy.

"Wh-what's this?" Champ asked.

"Y'all young niggas hit for a nice profit, huh? Murked a killa, too, huh? And what, y'all 'bout to split out that lil' change?" the big guy asked

"Man," Mel was the first to try to plead for his life and a way out of the situation. "It's not..."

"Nigga y'all robbed, though. See, me? I want his head, myself."

When the big guy spoke those words, he got an instant confused look from them. "Huh?" Tuck was confused.

"This nigga they call Pimp, some pretty boy-ass nigga," was the big guy's reply. It was a reply that stunned the three boys.

"Yeah, so if you looking for Pimp, then why you got us down bad?" Mel questioned.

"Y'all young niggas good by me. I just want him."

Big Dude reached down and tossed the bag at their feet.

"Keep ya earnings, and now you hired by me. Find that sucka, bring him to me, and we good."

Mel bent down, looked in the bag, and found everything was there.

"What beef you got with that nigga?" Champ asked.

"Pussy-nigga killed my baby ma, Taylor."

"Fine-ass Taylor?" Mel wanted to know. "You might be right, 'cause Murder Black got killed that same day and niggas saying he was behind that," Mel added.

"Yeah, I heard that same shit. Y'all niggas handle good business and I got y'all a good lump sum." The big dude and his six men left, releasing their auntie and her husband.

***

Icey, she knew love was real. She was feeling real love at the moment, but at the same time something felt out of place.

Driving home still fairly shaken by recent events, she pondered her next move. Savarous had finally opened up the truth, and she stuck her foot in her mouth by saying she was good with him, good or bad or through whatever.

Was she really down? One thing was for certain, she knew she was scared. In love, yeah, but scared as well. Just the possibility of what he was capable of tore at her mentally. But then his grace and charm, how humble he could be, it all overwhelmed her heart and granted her this unbelievable amount of joy.

The music played low in the car as she drove through Miami Beach, headed to the house. She wonder what time Pimp would be there, pondered how it would be around him after knowing the truth. He just didn't look the part he played. He fooled her good through mere charm, which she fell in love with.

Did he truly love her?

It was a question she now asked. It seems he did, but then again, did love have secrets? Did love have a closet filled with hands, holding the knob of truth? Preventing more truth from escaping? Icey didn't know, did not have the answers, but so badly wanted them.

She finally pulled up to the house, feeling some form of comfort just seeing her home minus the federal government. She parked in her spot and got out. The air was cool to her face as the wind blew lightly.

She was met at the door by the head cleaner, a Mexican woman who handled the other cleaners.

"Who's here?" Icey asked.

"No one, ma'am," the young Mexican woman spoke and took the bag from Icey.

"Okay." She walked into her home. Things were looking better as workers put her home in order. She made her way upstairs, not speaking to no one. She had one thing on her mind.

Icey went straight to the bedroom, her heart beating wildly in her chest. She closed and locked the door. With her back against the door, she just looked over the entire room. Everything looked in place.

She made her way over to his closet, moving slow while in deep thought. She just wanted to see his plan again. She wanted to really pay attention so she could know exactly what she was dealing with.

She entered the closet and moved his clothes to one side. She found the hidden latch and slid the door open, exposing the room. It was pitch black. With her free hand she reached inside for a light switch and found it on the wall.

She clicked the light on, and what she saw was nothing. The entire room was empty, nothing anywhere. She was confused.

She clicked the light off, slid the door back, and came out of the closet. Icey's mind was stuck all of a sudden. Had the feds found the room? She remembered it was there, so her mind wasn't playing tricks on her.

Icey rushed across the room to her phone. She needed to call Pimp to let him know what happened, or maybe he knew. She looked at her phone a moment longer and put it back down on the bed. Icey walked to the door, hands shaking, and unlocked it.

Downstairs she found the maid who cleaned their home daily. The woman was dusting the living room when Icey stopped at the top of the steps.

"Has Pimp been home? Have you seen him?" Icey asked.

"Yes, ma'am. Left about an hour ago. Said to tell you not to worry, and he'll be here by 9:00 p.m.," the maid informed her.

"Not to worry?"

"Yes, he said you may seek something, but will not find it. He said, but don't worry," the Mexican girl continued to dust as she was doing, leaving Icey stuck at the top of the steps, lost for words.

Icey walked back up to the bedroom. She got her phone and called Pimp. She needed to hear him say the words he sent as a message. Something wasn't right, and it was bothering her bad.

***

It was dark outside on Pine Street. It would've been darker if the streetlights didn't give it a glow. Junkies came and went, young dealers walked back and forth, and every now and then a fancy car or two would pass through the block.

Tonight the trap was jumping. Somebody had put some good dope in the streets.

"Say, miss lady, c'mere," a voice spoke from the shadows as a basehead was walking by. Her attention was across the street, looking at a group of young knotheads and females. The lady was high out of her mind, it seemed like, and was trying to find another blast. She looked up toward the voice as if she was hearing something until the voice spoke again.

"Over here."

This time she saw him in the darkness. "What's up, nephew?"

"Got what you looking for, Auntie. C'mere."

The high basehead made her way over through greed, not caring if she would be killed or not. "What's good, nephew? Watcha got?"

"Here." He gave her three sacks of crack rock. "I need some information."

"What information?" the basehead asked the man hidden in the shadows. It didn't stop her from accepting the rocks.

"I'm looking for a few niggas, maybe you can help. Best believe it's more where that came from," he pointed to the rocks in her hand.

"Who you looking for, honey? I been 'round here for thirty years. Lil' bit know everybody, honey, from the mamma to the grandbabies." The basehead rocked back and forth, fumbling with her rocks.

***

Meanwhile, Mel had walked inside the trap house on Pine Street, leaving both Champ and Tuck posted. Tonight it was cool, just the hood doing what the hood did best. Music blasted from one of the many cars posting the block and females walked between any hustlers that played the sidewalk.

"Somebody give me a wrap so I can roll up," Champ yelled over the music to anybody, it didn't matter. Right then he felt like the man of the year. After he and his cousins split the money and each got a brick, Champ instantly felt rich and wanted more, so that was his plan from then on.

"Here, meaning I'm in on it." One of their Pine Street homies gave Champ the blunt wrap he was looking for.

"You know it," Champ boasted.

Three females were walking by when he stepped out and grabbed the thicker one's arm "What yo' name?" Champ was all over the girl. He was the man in his hood.

She had to know who he was and what he was about.

She slightly pulled her arm from his grip, but stopped and spoke. "My name is Naomi."

"Oh, yeah? And you don't know me?" he asked.

"Yeah, I heard of you a time or two"

"Okay then. Well, shoot me yo' number so I can make you number one and only."

When he said that, she blushed. "We can do that." Naomi wrote her number down, then left with her friends.

Tuck was already captivated by a honey sitting between his legs.

Neither guy knew their lives were in danger. Neither knew what lay in the darkness for them was death with a clip. All Champ and his cousin knew was they had a job to do, and they would get paid to do it. Pimp was a dead man walking. It was only a matter of time before they faced off with him, and when it popped off, it was gonna be ugly.

Champ rolled the blunt up and got out of the street.

"Yo, what the hell wrong with Auntie? Bitch ova dere talking to herself," Champ said, looking at a basehead across the street. She was a known junkie who'd been around since he could remember. Nobody paid her attention, they just let Auntie do her.

"You know that woman nuts," Tuck said, and just as he spoke the words, Auntie lit up a hit of her pipe right there beside the building, in plain view.

"Where that nigga Mel at? I'm surprised he not tryna put his money in the bank." Champ laughed at his own joke as if it was funny. It sounded so stupid even Tuck smiled, but didn't get it.

***

Across the street, Auntie hit the crack rock given to her by the man in the shadows. Her ears were ringing, her eyes saw stars, and she was higher than a plane.

"Who? Who you? Who?" The crack had her stuck. "Who you wanna find, baby?" She started touching her pockets, then looking around. Her eyes were stoned and wide, and she was speaking slow.

The shadow smirked, knowing the affect his drug had on people. "I'm looking for a kid name Champ"

"Champ?" The basehead thought for a minute. She turned and looked over her shoulder, then looked at the shadow, but this time he had emerged a bit. He was a kid himself.

"Champ is the one standing over there with the green shirt on. Give Auntie another one of them thangs, now." The basehead held out her hand.

He reached in his pocket and gave her a couple more sacks. He tossed his hoodie on and jumped on the bike he rode. Cranking it up with his helmet on, he pulled off into the road and mashed down Pine Street.

"Who da fuck?" Champ was caught off guard when the motorcycle crunk up and peeled off. Tuck also stood up, looking down the street in the direction the motorcycle went.

"Who was that, yo?"

"I'on know. Da nigga was in the cut over there by Auntie high ass," Champ said, looking back across the street, but Auntie was gone.

"Where that bitch at?" Tuck wanted to know.

"Her ass was just there, probably in the cut. Let's go find her."

Champ and Tuck were both feeling strange.

Something wasn't right with that picture, they both agreed to that. Across the street, it only took the boys ten seconds to find Auntie sitting on a crate behind a trash bin. She looked up fearful from a blast off her pipe, a cloud of white smoke covered her face.

"What's up, nephew?"

"Who that dude was that rode off on that bike a minute ago?" Tuck asked Auntie, fanning the rising smoke out of his face.

"Oh, some young fella looking for you," she pointed to Champ.

"How he look?" Champ questioned.

"Lil' red dude, baby-face fella. Honey, I can't remember. All you look the same, Auntie be so high."

Tuck and Champ walked off. They knew it could only be that nigga Pimp.

"Go grab Mel. I'm going to get the whip," Tuck told Champ, who agreed. If Pimp wanted to roll up on their block, they could do the same. But they would make something happen, not pump fake it.

Jerry Jackson

Chapter Four

Set Up a Trap

Donte and his crew of two shooters were posted in two different houses on the block. One house sat next to the blue store. It was empty and hadn't had life in it for more than thirty years.

Donte was hidden in the window with his choppa ready. His two shooters were across the street in another house that was abandoned. They were also posted in the windows with their choppas.

Montay was out handling the club business, and Pimp was posted inside the blue store with a few workers. He knew it was only a matter of time before Champ and his boys pull up on some young nigga shit, and Pimp had plans to make them pay for it.

Ashley and Cindy were walking into the store when a black Ford pickup truck rounded the corner. It seemed like everything came to a slow creep. Pimp was on point as the truck turned the corner. Three guys on the back rose up, all holding guns, but before they could act on their mission, bullets struck them.

Boom boom, boom boom, boom boom.

Shots rang from either side of the street. The truck slammed into a pole up the street, and people screamed and ran for their lives.

"Bitch-ass niggas," Pimp said with a wicked smile on his face. He came out of the store and jumped into his Benz. He pulled off, laughing to himself hard. Miami wasn't ready for him and most of his ways. The young dudes most def didn't know how to handle him.

This should teach the Pine Hill niggas a lesson or two.

Queen was a good nigga, and good niggas didn't get murdered without repercussions.

Pimp's mind instantly went to Icey and wondered what she was doing, how she was holding up, and how was their unborn child? Out of all the situations he has faced, this was the only issue that confused him, the only thing that had him baffled. Love wasn't that real, or was it? *It can't be possible*, he thought with a shake of his head.

His cell phone started ringing at the same time the Benz came to a stop at NW 63rd Street. Pimp looked down and it was a text message from Chino. It read:

I just saw Champ and his cousins, they riding around in a Charger

Pimp knew that was impossible 'cause he just saw three niggas get murdered on the block. Three niggas who had guns and were ready to use them had to be them lil' niggas.

Just before Pimp was about to text him back, something told him to look up, and that's when he caught 'em. Champ was in the car next to him. He jumped out, and he and another dude tried to jump in the Benz. The door was locked, preventing them from getting in. Both boys had guns and didn't use them.

Pimp reacted quickly as Champ busted the passenger window with his gun. Pimp picked up his Breta and aimed and shot, but Champ fell back to the ground. Pimp turned the gun on the other dude, who was also ducking. The light turned green, so Pimp pulled off into traffic.

"What the hell?" Pimp laughed while looking in the rearview. The boys didn't follow him. He wondered why, but most importantly he wondered why they didn't just roll up and bust. They had him down bad and did not act on it. Who were the other three niggas Donte and his crew murked? That had Pimp baffled. He shook his head, looked at the rearview again, and mashed the gas a little harder than the first time.

***

She felt his presence without her eyes open and with her back to the door. She could feel him standing there. It wasn't really late, but she was in the bed, tired. Being pregnant proved to be far more challenging than she thought, plus all the things going on had her emotions all over the place.

Icey didn't stir, didn't speak a word. She just listened to him move around in their bedroom, her eyes remained closed, in fear of opening. The bed moved, the covers were pulled back, and her eyes remain closed. She could feel him next to her, but not touching her as she longed to be.

Did he not love her anymore? She knew he didn't trust her, but did he hate her already?

She wanted to cry, but she was scared his hate was so strong it wasn't gonna be like it once was.

She felt his touch right at the moment she was about to say something. His hand was cold. The sensation and the coldness made chills run through her body. His hand gripped her thigh lightly and pulled her to him. Icey nested under him as his hand landed on her stomach. She took his hand and smiled because God must have heard her prayer and knew she was scared.

"How you feeling, baby girl?" Pimp said low, more

into her neck than her ear.

"Me and the baby are better now that you're home," she quickly replied.

"Icey, look at me," said Pimp. He let her go so she could turn to face him. She did, and she saw the man she was madly in love with. Pimp reached up to her face and moved a strand of her hair.

"Baby," she was about to speak.

"I love you, Icey," he cut her off.

"I love you, Savarous," she softly replied, as humble as he did.

Pimp lightly brushed the side of her face with his thumb. He smiled just a bit, then said, "I believe you. I see yo' innocence, Icey, but at the same time you are committed to a friendship that was many, many years before me. But I, too, see yo' love for –"

He couldn't finish his statement because she put her finger to his lips. She kissed his hand on her face and said, "I'll never let a friendship dictate my elevation in life. I have your child, Savarous. I have your heart, and don't nothing compare to that. I will not let Brad hold me back."

Those were words spoken from her heart. She knew deep down she was being open and honest. She just hoped he believed her.

Pimp didn't say anything at first. It was like his thoughts were adding up, so he just looked at her for a moment. His face didn't give off any signs; his expression was just something like plain and humble.

"Like I said, Icey, I believe you. Though, if you fail me…"

"I won't fail you!" She was determined for him to know.

"I'm just saying, I'm willing to take that chance."

"It's not a chance," she cut him off.

"Okay, baby, you win." He laughed when he said it.

"I win you, 'cause you all I want," Icey replied, then they kissed. Pimp pulled her closer to him. She threw one of her legs over his own as he took a handful of booty and gripped it.

Icey only had on some panties and a t-shirt. Pimp had on boxers. His dick found its way out and hardened due to the embrace. She felt him press to her, so with one free hand she grabbed his dick. Icey loved its feeling, its warmth. They continued to kiss, but now she slowly stroked his hardness back and forth, tasting his tongue, loving their moment.

With her hand gripping him, Pimp kind of moved to a rhythm, then took her leg from over him and turned her to her back. Even through the darkness he could see her beauty as he pushed up her shirt up exposing her cute chest and sexy stomach. Pimp kissed her stomach, at the same time pulling her panties down to her ankles. He kissed her hip bone, then kissed and sucked her inner thigh.

Icey bit her lip and opened her legs wide. His tongue found her wetness, which made her jump from the amazing sensation. She tasted sweet. Pimp sucked some of her wetness into his mouth, then trapped her clit with his tongue and tips. With a mouthful of her juices, he let it run over her pussy as his tongue moved slow circles on her clit.

Icey held his head with one hand and palmed her breast. She squeezed her breast and slightly rolled her hips.

Pimp rubbed her other breast with one hand and held

her legs more open with the other as he ate her good and slow. Tears were in her eyes as love warmed her body. She was in love with this man and wanted nothing but him.

Icey felt her body tense up. She gripped his head as she felt herslef about to cum.

Pimp knew this was when she came. He could always tell by the way her body moved. He sucked her clit more, moving his tongue side-to-side and pushing a finger into her.

"I'm. I'm 'bout. I'm cumming!" Icey screamed out her pleasure as her body shook. Pimp made sure he tasted her flavor, and with one last kiss he came up from between her legs. He slid up her stomach with kisses, then found himself face-to-face with her.

Icey sucked on Pimp's bottom lip. Pimp sucked on her top and slid his hardness into her wet pussy. She was so warm, so pretty, and fit him like a glove. In and out Pimp went with passion-filled strokes that touched her deep enough to steal a mean and firm backrub from her.

Pimp was in love, Icey was in love, and they felt it in the embrace of their lovemaking. Even their bodies moved together as one, only making this love they felt for one another more real than seemed possible. Pimp stroked and kissed her at the same time. He felt so at peace between her legs. It felt so good feeling her wrapped around him that he couldn't help but cum inside her. He came slow and grinding while kissing so his body shook as she sucked his tongue into her mouth. Pimp gripped her hips and kept grinding as his cum poured into her.

"I love you so much," said Icey.

"I love you as well, babygirl," Pimp nearly moaned his reply.

***

The next day Pimp was on his A-game moving through the Miami streets. He knew he couldn't slip at all 'cause every step counted. Now he needed some understanding from the streets, plus he had something nice for Champ and his bitch-ass crew.

Times and situations like this were those moments when Pimp got what he could out of the state he was in and found another home. But first things first, his beef would be handled.

He wouldn't just leave Icey, and he knew she couldn't or wouldn't just pack up and leave, either. He would deal with these issues head-on, not walk away from them like many times in the past.

Pulling up in a midnight-black Charger with heavy tints, Donte and one of his gunners was standing out at the blue store. He also saw Montay's Benz parked out front.

Pimp jumped out, like always clean in some Guess jeans, Jordans, and a North Carolina blue shirt with his hometown stamped on the front. He wore no hat, just his waves spinning deep in his jet-black hair.

"What's up, my nigga?" Pimp asked, then pounded both Donte and his gunner.

"'Sup, big homie? We out he'e, posted," Dontae shot back.

"Where Montay at? In the store?"

"Yeah, bruh just pulled up."

Pimp walked into the blue store that had a few people shopping for weight. Armed men were posted at the door, but didn't bother Pimp, knowing who he was. Pimp walked to the back where he found Montay counting some money on the machine. Montay looked up through his Gucci frames.

"What it do, bruh?"

"Shid, just pulling up. Any more word on Champ? Or who the fuck that was who sent three niggas 'round here to die?" Pimp asked.

"Nothing 'bout who them cats was, and as far as Champ 'n them going, I got an eye on one of them fools. Mel, he fucks with a lil' female, I be fucking her best friend. We can catch him with his drawe's down," Montay informed Pimp with a slick smile. Pimp nodded his head in agreement because the plan sounded good.

"I'm still tryna figure why they didn't bust, though. Them fuck-niggas had me down bad, bruh, and fuck round and let up. I tried to dead them hos and got out of there."

Pimp thought about last night. He had many enemies, but most were dead or in other states. Somebody wanted him alive, not dead, was his thoughts. But *why* was the big question. Pimp would find out one way or another, 'cause they didn't want him dead, but he wanted their life in his hand, under good belt.

"I don't know why they spared you, but I'm glad they did. We'll run the info down on them niggas before they know it. We almost out of blow, too," Montay shot back while still counting money. Chino walked in with a classic Gucci bag over his shoulder.

"Big home," he acknowledged Pimp, then sat the bag on the table. It was filled with money, Pimp noticed.

"'Sup? Okay, say around six, you'll be straight?" Pimp told Montay.

"I'll be in the club by then, bruh."

"Well, Donte gon' get it handled," assured Pimp. He

stayed another second in the blue store, then he walked back out to Donte.

"What's up with any word about last night?" Pimp pulled up and laughed when he thought about some niggas trying to snatch him up.

"Some shit 'bout niggas paid to catch you, kill you, or some shit. Fuck 'em though, big homie. We all will die out here if you go," Donte said and meant it.

"Fuck yeah, these niggas going, too. Couple police, too. I'on give two fucks if niggas think they can just snatch me up. Niggas done messed around and let the size fool them." Pimp was serious, too, and Donte knew it.

"I'm witcha, big homie, trust that," Donte said, looking up and down the street while crack sales were being made. Traffic was thick today, early.

"You know I know," Pimp told him while he, too, looked down the block to see nothing out of place.

Icey crossed his mind at that moment, and he wondered how she was feeling? Was she still asleep, or woke and thinking about him? However it go, she was on his mind heavy. Pimp knew he was playing with fire, but he was in love and couldn't help his own actions.

Pimp gave Donte another pound, then walked off saying, "I'ma hit yo' line in a minute, bruh"

"Bet that," replied Donte.

After leaving Pokey Bean Projects, Pimp had a meeting with one of his father's lawyers. She was an older white woman who almost always flirted with him, or better yet, threw her pussy at him. Pimp always kept clean, though, and never messy.

Her name was Tiffany Gray. She was forty-six and fit to a tee with a made-up face of makeup. Ms. Gray was the type of woman who wore a lot of jewelry, expensive clothes, and loud perfume that always smelled sweet. She was beautiful, hands-down, and most importantly she was helping his father.

The meeting was scheduled to take place at an expensive restaurant nearby. It didn't take him long at all to find the place she chose. After parking his car and double-checking himself, making sure he was strapped, Pimp entered the restaurant.

Pimp found her at their table already. She had her iPad with her and was typing when he walked up

"What's up, Ms. Gray?"

"What I tell you 'bout that, Savarous?" she said without looking up from her iPad.

Pimp took his seat. "Respect, that's all."

"Understood." Then she jumped straight to business. "So, listen. In order for your father to get another trial, nine judges must sign off on the papers. So far we have eight that have signed over the past four years. It's just Judge Emerson who's being hard-pressed that your father don't get another trial," the lawyer explained.

"And without him signing the paper, then it's no trial?" asked Pimp, trying to understand exactly what she was talking about.

"Correct."

"What do he want? Money? I mean, what's our options?" Pimp wanted to know. He was willing to do anything.

"Well, your dad has been in prison over twenty years. Mr. Emerson was old then, so you know he's old now. Only way your father could get a trial without Mr. Emerson is his death, so I say we build our case the next few years, and by then Mr. Emerson will pass. With him out of the picture, we got a trial," the lawyer told him.

"I like that. Yeah, okay, cool," Pimp replied, mind already racing miles per second thinking of something to fix the situation.

"Well, it's settled 'cause in court we will eat them alive. Everyone that was involved in your father's case except the governor of Carolina is dead. All got murdered over the time," the lawyer told Pimp, who nodded his head that he understood.

After the quick evening meal, he walked her to her car and, like always, she tried to get slick with him.

"You can pick up the phone, too, sometimes. Am I that old?" She was serious, but acted as if she was joking.

"I gotcha, Ms. Gray," Pimp assured her.

"I hope you do."

Jerry Jackson

Chapter Five

The Introduction

His name was Melvin. His wife called him Melvin, his kids called him Daddy, and his grandkids call him Papa. He had no friends to call him nothing at all because with him everything was business. With every business deal made, he was the winner. Every situation he came out on top, either right or wrong.

Nobody understood him. No one knew him. All they saw was this 6'9", midnight-black dude who was vicious, and his name was Devil.

Devil was seated comfortably in the backseat of his S600 Maybach V12, talking business on his phone. For the past week he'd been staying in Miami in his penthouse for the petty reason of murdering Pimp himself. Usually Devil staid off the scene. He was a family guy, a big business owner who ran the streets from his mind, using other niggas' muscles to do his dirty work. Devil bought off half the city storefronts and thirty percent of the homes t in Miami. He paid for everything in cash out of his pocket from drug money.

Now he was out and about, lurking the Miami streets in search of Pimp himself. It seemed none of the niggas he sent to snatch Pimp could make it happen. It seemed niggas was either scared or rookies.

Seated next to Devil was his young, tender, twenty-six year old, exotic-looking female named Cake, but there wasn't nothing sweet about her and her short height. She was as viscious as her man. She continue to sit there while Devil conducted his business over the phone. The Benz turned on 63rd NW, a place Pimp hung.

As the Benz rode up the block, Cake gripped her Dracko 50. Devil continue talking as they came up to a blue store with a Benz parked out front, a Range Rover, and some more whips. There was a few dudes posted out front, but only two stood out to Cake. She tapped Devil's shoulder.

"Yes, pretty?" he looked over at her, pulling the phone away from his ear.

She pointed. "We here."

That's when Devil finally paid attention.

The Benz came to a stop, and the driver turned around and looked at his boss. "Now what, sir?"

Devil, still seated comfortably, followed Cake's pointing fingers and saw what she saw. He put the phone back to his ear.

"I'll make a decision later tonight and call you then," Devil said into the phone. He nodded his head twice to whatever the other end was saying, then hung up.

Meanwhile, Donte saw when the Maybach pulled up and rode slowly down the block. His bretta in close reach, he wasn't worried at all. And when he saw a dude and a bitch in the back, he was really good.

The Benz stopped in front of the store, a few feet away from where he and his gunner stood. Donte eased his hand to his back pocket while watching the two in the backseat, not worried about the driver. He wondereed who this dude was, because he was looking lost and out of place with his bitch.

Donte wondered what they wanted, and just when he was about to say something about it to his gunner, the window to the Benz rolled down just a crack and the girl spoke.

"Yo, sexy. Sexy, come here real fast," she said. Donte

stepped off the curb into the streets, his hand still at his back pocket where his gun was ready. He saw the dude was a big black nigga, sitting back in his seat as the female leaned up. "Who running this block?" the girl asked.

"Why?" Now Donte gripped his gun.

"'Cause my man wanna know who he need to hire, if you know what I mean," she winked.

Donte wasn't feeling her vibe at all, and he felt something wasn't right. "Yo' man?" he asked, then looked over his shoulder to his gunner. He ment for him to join them.

"Yeah, me," the big guy finally spoke as the window came down a little more. Donte's gunner stood at his side.

"I run this block. What's up?" Donte shot back.

"So, you're the man I'm looking for? But the thing is, you are not this short, skinny dude with red skin. I'm looking for Pimp. Is that you?" the big guy spoke.

When the words left his lips, she notice the guy outside her window tense up. His hand was hidden behind his back, and she knew he was strapped. His other friend stood to the side, also, with a gun tucked but hands close by. Cake knew something was about to happen. She could feel it.

Before Cake could react, all she saw was quick movement. The first dude came from behind his back with a gun. Cake began to raise her gun, but Devil, being the thinker, rolled up the windows as the guy and his gunner both aimed and shot.

Cake jumped as the bullets struck and bounced off the window.

Boom, boom, boom, boom, boom, boom, boom, boom.

All Devil did was look at the guys' faces, then told

his driver, "Pull off."

***

It was a sad day in North Carolina. Yolanda had been down and out since hearing the news yesterday about Diamond and her unborn son. The news clearly showed Pimp as the killer. Yolanda knew for a fact it was Pimp. He always was one to do something so stupid. She really disliked Pimp.

The moment she watched the news name Shawn, AKA Shaw, as Diamond's killer, she wondered how Pimp pulled that one off. What reason did he have to just kill that poor girl?

Over the past months, Yolanda found out Diamond was just a young female who was in love with Pimp. He was her dream come true, and he took her life for it. Just the thought alone bothered Yolanda. Her heart went out to Diamond and her family.

She clicked off the TV inside of the doctor's waiting area. She no longer worked at CVS. She was now working at a private doctor's office and was in love with her job.

She sat the remote down and was just about to walk out when three FBI agents walked in and straight up to her. Yolanda was lost at first because she was no criminal. The feds pulled out some pictures of Pimp, and she looked at for a moment.

"What's this?" she asked.

"Your ex-boyfriend, Savarous Jones, AKA Pimp. The two of you stayed together a few months back," one of the agents said.

"And?" was Yolanda's only reply. She knew she

wasn't in trouble with the law, plus she'd never helped Pimp, or for that matter, was down with any of his crimes. All she had was love for Pimp. He was her man at the time, so back then she supported him as expected.

"We have some questions to ask about Savarous. It would be great if we could borrow your time," one of the agents said.

"What can I tell you that's helpful? I don't know any of his business, so what do you want?" Yolanda said.

"Answer this: do you know of any crime Savarous could have or did commit when you two was together? You will not get into any trouble if so."

"I've never known Savarous to do crime, never seen nor heard stories of him doing anything illegal," Yolanda lied with a straight face the agents couldn't read well.

Even though she really disliked Pimp at the moment, she still couldn't snitch on him. She just couldn't be the reason he went down, plus she had recently received a letter from Pimp's father asking her to stick around because he knew she and Pimp would be together. This gave her all the good news she needed to hear, and gave her all the hope one person could hold in one day.

"Well, we find that hard to believe being that your signature is on his bond paperwork. Why protect someone who isn't even with you anymore? Didn't he just up and leave you?" The feds were clearly getting frustrated with her.

"I can't remember any of what you're saying. Like I said, Savarous has never did wrong from what I've seen."

When she said the words, one of the agents started writing something in a folder. The taller one rolled his eyes, face turning red, and walked off while the older agent stood there. He was trying to read Yolanda. He knew she was lying, knew she was hiding something. All he wanted to know was what.

Shortly after the FBI left, she went to the back and called Pimp. She had to let him know what was up. The phone rang a few times before his voicemail picked up. She left him a detailed message telling him what was going on.

Yolanda badly wanted to say something about Diamond, but she decided to wait for another day and time. She hung up the phone, then returned to work with so much on her mind, but mainly Pimp.

***

Mel was the one out of the three cousins who did most of the thinking. He was the older and more calm soul, rather than Champ and Tuck, who were two wild hotheads always ready to do something stupid. Mel was rolling a morning blunt after he finally woke up from a deep sleep, his baby mother was at work, and her eight-year brother was in the living room playing a game 'cause it was loud, as always. He could hear the NBA live.

After the blunt was rolled, Mel put some fire to it and inhaled a thick cloud of smoke.

Mel was one of them guys who thought a lot about everything. At the same time, he hardly ever thought to take action. One thing for certain, two things for sure: his daughter was important, so the things he did from now on had to be done with sense.

Champ and Tuck were gonna get themselves killed before it was over with, and that's something Mel wanted to stay away from. They were never supposed to kill Queen, but it happened. The plan was simply to rob him and get out of there, but Champ and Tuck both wanted to prove a point.

Mel was never down for murder, and he most def wasn't down for the Big Guy and his plan to kidnap Pimp.

Last night when they tried to snatch Pimp up, they could have got murdered 'cause Pimp didn't hesitate to pop it off in traffic and pulled off. Mel wanted to chill with his earnings. He would sell the kilo in nickle sacks until it was all gone and let his two cousins handle that Rambo shit.

He smoked the whole blunt, then grabbed his phone off the nightstand to check his missed calls and messages. All the calls were from Champ, and a few *Get@me* texts.

He put the lil' blunt in the ashtray and stood up. He tossed the phone on the bed and walked out of the room where his baby mother's brother was playing the video game.

Mel's heart fell to the pit of his stomach when he opened the door and saw a blood trail from the bathroom to the living room. He quickly ran back into his room to grab his gun.

"What the fuck!" was all Mel could say as he started to panic. He rushed back to the door and followed the blood splatter. When Mel saw just the feet of his baby mother, his heart was crushed. She had been stabbed a couple times. She lay next to her little brother, who was sitting up with his eyes opened wide, a look of terror in his dead eyes. His throat had been slit.

How did I sleep through this? was Mel's thought as he broke down crying, then called the cops. He was glad his daughter wasn't home.

Mel got up to look around the house. He needed to leave, but knew he couldn't, so he hid his gun and then thought about the kilo of coke. He didn't find it in the room where he knew it was, but did find the bag it was in plus all the money missing. Mel felt faint.

***

Donte called Pimp to the duck-off spot because they needed to talk and doing so over the phone was a no-no. Pimp pulled up in his Benz and jumped out to a crowd of niggas in the yard and on the porch. Donte wore no shirt when he walked up to Pimp. Everyone looking at the two.

"Just had to pop it off on some nigga and his bitch pulling up on the Block, asking 'bout you and shit. Man. this nigga riding around in a bulletproof Benz, big homie. This nigga didn't even flinch when I whipped out and bust. Bullets popping right off his shit. Maybach bulletproof," Donte told Pimp, who was surprised by the news himself.

"Oh, word? Who was this dude?"

"Fuck yeah. Montay closed the entire store down. Fuck it, police third time out there, each time gunshots, niggas shot and murdered. Montay, we sitting ducks for the cops," Donte shot back quick.

"He right. Go get that money and blow out the car. Let's go count this shit," Pimp told Donte, then walked into the trap house. Pimp took out his own phone while taking a seat on the arm of a chair. He played a message from Yolanda saying the feds was in town with his pictures, asking questions. This was a message he wasn't sure he wanted to hear. What the fuck was the feds doing up there?

He called Montay, who picked up the line on the third ring. "Yeah?"

"What's good, bruh?" Pimp asked

"That business been handled. I got that brick back and some money, but change of plans. I had to off that young nigga, Tuck, and his lil' girlfriend, so Pine Street hot," Montay said.

"Okay, cool. That's two down, one to go. So listen, tap in with yo' intel and see who got enough paper to ride around bulletproof. Donte said some black-ass nigga," Pimp told him 'cause this situation had to be handled. No nigga would press him and not get the pressure back.

"Okay, bet that. I shut down the store, too, 'cause that entire spot on fire."

"Yeah, Donte told me. That's good thinking. I gotta figure this nigga out who riding around looking for me." Pimp was seriously considering going back to the hot spots to turn some rocks himself to see who this dude was.

"Shid, we got 'em. Just give me a minute to put some calls together," Montay told him, and Pimp hesitantly agreed.

"Big homie, this ain't but nineteen racks," Donte told Pimp, pointing to the money.

"Cool. Bust that brick down real quick and pull up on yo' people wit' it, then we'll link up later," Pimp told Donte, then he left the spot with his mind on murder and money.

***

His mother, his aunties, his whole family was crushed. Tragedy had hit home with his family, and Champ was at blame. Mel was at blame, but their families didn't know.

Champ was at a hotel, hiding from the work. Didn't

nobody know where he was but GG, his baby. Tonight he planned to find and murder Pimp 'cause he knew it was him. Mel had been blowing him up wanting to ride, too, but Champ ignored his calls.

He was hurt by his cousin Tuck and his Aunt Patti. She took it hard. Champ was wishing they never pulled the stunt 'cause he was missing his cousin already. Blunt in one hand and drink in the other, Champ sat at the table. Gun on the table. Phone on the table. He would only text GG, nobody else.

GG was a mother of one with one on the way, pretty brown skin tone, short and thick. Most niggas complemented her sexy, full lips and cat-like eyes. She was that thick-fine that niggas liked. She had the right size and shape with the ass and breasts to match and a face of an angel.

At that very moment she wore no pretty look, no sexy clothes. Right then she was sitting at home with her child while texting Champ back and forth, scared for his life. Champ robbed the wrong people this time 'cause war had hit home, and it seemed wasn't nobody safe. She had constantly begged Champ to give the man his money and drugs back. She asked him to move out of state and she'd go with him, but he refused to leave, and look what happened.

When will I see you?

GG sent the text. Her daughter was asleep lying next to her, so when she heard something up front, she got up out of the bed. The last thing she expected was some mad man kicking in her door to harm her and her daughter for something he did.

Idk.

She saw Champ's reply. She put the phone down and

left the room. She checked the living room and saw the door was open. And then she saw him standing there.

GG didn't know what to think, what move to make, or what to say as she watched this dude stand in her kitchen with a gun in his hand. At first she thought he was a child when she looked at him, but the way he was holding that gun made her realize she was dealing with a grown man.

"If you don't wanna get hurt, you need to tell me where my blow at and exactly where to find ya boy, Champ," the guy spoke, and GG knew he was serious.

True indeed, she loved Champ and was down with him, but their daughter meant more. GG didn't hesitate.

"It's in my room. Take it. But I don't know where to find Champ, I swear to God."

"Bitch, stop lyin'! Take me to my shit." He forcefully pushed her into the room.

GG quickly found the kilo of dope and gave it up with tears in her eyes.

"Now call that nigga."

She knew Champ would be mad she gave up his stash, but every time she looked down to her baby in her bed, she knew what she was doing was right. She called Champ like the dude told her to.

"Wassup?"

"Thank you, fuck-nigga," Pimp said, then lifted his gun to the girl's face. GG wanted to scream, but at the same time she wanted to try to talk him out of doing something stupid. She was about to say something when the loud bang and bright flash came that ended her life. GG had no more thoughts as her body hit the ground.

He looked at the baby in bed, asleep still. And just as he came, he left.

Jerry Jackson

Chapter Six

Money Wins Wars, Peace Can't Buy

Roxy was a slim-fine. She had nice hips and a just the right booty. She stood about 5'7" with baseball-size breasts. Riggs was short, but also slim with exotic features about her. She was red with tattoos all over her sexy, fun-size shape. Riggs had long hair that all the girls swore was fake 'cause it reached her butt, which was fat, but fake. Nyia was a soft-looking redbone with a deep tan. Her eyes were sexy, and so was her body. She was a workout freak, so her body was toned good, and that's something Big Guy liked.

Roxy was between his legs, stroking his dick – a big dick they called a monster. None of the girls could handle Big Guy, but they all tried. She used both hands and stroked his dick, using only her lips and a lot of saliva on his head as she stroked him. This technique Big Guy loved, and Roxy was loving the feeling on Nyia's tongue as it danced around her pussy walls.

"Yes, baby, eat this candy," Riggs said while squatting down over Big Guy's face. She was his favorite. All the girls were strippers who worked at different clubs Big Guy paid good money to party with.

Big Guy gripped her booty as he tongue-fucked her fat pussy that always tasted sweet. Roxy put his dickhead in her mouth and started jacking him harder, and Big Guy rotated his hips. All he could hear was smacking and moaning as they had a foursome.

Nyia was a pro at eating pussy because that's all she ever liked to do. She was the type of female who could do without the dick. Just give her some pussy and she was good.

She stuck her tongue deep into Roxy and made it dance as she held Roxy in place.

Roxy felt like she had died and gone to heaven. She sucked and stroked Big Guy's 13-inch monster cock, tasting his precum.

Big Guy slapped Riggs on her booty once she came in his mouth. He swallowed all her flavor, then she got up. Big Guy pulled Roxy up his body, then slid his member inside her. Roxy wasn't small, but she was slim and her pussy was tight. She closed her eyes tight as his dickhead entered her. Nyia rubbed his thighs and balls, at the same time holding his shaft in place as Roxy tried to ride him. Big Guy rubbed both her breasts while Riggs stood over him, rubbing her pussy.

Big Guy was a rich man and spent his money well on things he wanted. Cake sat in the corner of the room and watched her man's back, holding her Drako eyes on the only door a nigga could come through. Most bitches would have been highly jealous seeing their man fuck three bad bitches at the same time, but Cake was a real down ho who knew how to play the game. She eyed Riggs, who was a short redbone Cake wanted to taste herself 'cause the lil' bitch had swagg.

After about an hour of fucking and sucking, Big Guy finally made the three strippers leave, and then he joined her in the corner.

"What's word, baby girl?" Big Guy was still naked.

Cake paid him no mind as she showed him a picture of the block he ordered hit. Big Guy had men sent out to kill everything in Pokey Bean Project that was moving. He sent the hit out to make sure niggas knew who they was dealing with so the next time he pulled up, they'd show respect.

"That's done," Cake said.

"Good," Big Guy replied. Pimp wouldn't make it far. Big Guy haven't even turned up the juice yet and already done killed up half Pimp's block. Murder brought the police and the police brought a problem, so he had to be messing with Pimp's pockets. He couldn't hustle, and hustling was all Pimp had.

"He also got ties to this club downtown," Cake said, knowing if the club failed, then Pimp was really dead.

"Let him have that. I'm doing good to keep the violence down. Don't forget this half my city. I'll only be hurting myself," Big Guy told her so she would better understand.

"Okay, I see," Cake replied.

"Anyways, my beef is directly to him. That stunt last night in the projects was just to show the hood I'm still vicious. I only want Pimp life for killing Taylor and leaving my kids without a mother, but after this I'm going back to my business. Baby, trust me when I say it's far more life than this pretty kid." Big Guy got dressed as he told Cake his plan. She listened like the boss she was. She knew the deal, and like always, she was down for him.

Everything Big Guy rode in was bulletproof, so everywhere he went, he went solo. Just him, his driver, and a bitch mostly, but tonight he had two carloads of niggas with him. He would personally hunt Pimp down and murder him for what he did to Taylor.

Inside his bulletproof Bentley, he and Cake sat comfortably, ready to pull out. One car in front of him, one car at the back is how he told his crew because it was about to go down in Miami.

***

Champ had to fix his mind that what he heard on the other end of the phone was a joke or trick or something. It couldn't be true that Pimp had found his girl's crib, and it wasn't true he actually shot GG. It could not be.

Champ was blowing her phone up, though, and got no answer, which only worried him more. He had to get out of the hotel and see for himself what was up.

His family was still hurt by him allowing his cousin to be killed, so really Champ had nothing to live for is how he was feeling. He grabbed his gun and what money he had. About to call his aunt, he decided against it as he proceeded out the door, murder on his mind. Who was that guy, Pimp? It was a big mistake to mess with him or anyone with him. Champ wasn't no scary dude, plus he had a bigger heart than he would admit to. But at the same time he had enough common sense to know when he could win or not win a war in the streets. One thing he wouldn't do is tuck his tail. He wasn't a ho by far, so one day he'd face Pimp or any other nigga. It didn't bother him about being killed. What bothered him was his family being hurt behind his mess.

Champ wouldn't know what to do if something happened to his daughter or GG. Already failing to save Tuck, he vowed to let nobody else get hurt.

Once inside the whip, Lucci boomed through the speakers as he pulled off, headed to GG's house. It took him nearly an hour to pull up on her street, and when he did, his worst fear was confirmed. Police were everywhere with crime scene tape surrounding the house. Champ was so shocked he stopped the car two houses down from GG's house. He jumped out with tears already falling out of his eyes.

It took a few police officers to hold him back as he desperately tried to get through to the house.

"Let me go! My daughter! Where is my daughter? Let me go!" Champ yelled as the tears fell.

"Hold on, sir. Hold –"

"I got 'im. Let him go." A white dude who stood 6'8" lifted up the yellow tape. He was the lead detective who Champ knew all too well. The officers let Champ go.

"My daughter, she's –"

"She's fine. Come with me."

The detective's name was Johnson. Champ followed him over to a van, eyes carefully scanning the crowd of people looking for his baby mother. He saw some of her family crying and falling out all over the place, which panicked him even more.

"Johnson, what's up, man? What's going on?" Champ couldn't help but ask.

Johnson turned around and faced him. Out of all the times he'd locked Champ up, out of all the sad days the family had dealing with Johnson, this time was a tough one. He didn't want to be the one to tell Champ his daughter's mother had been murdered.

Detective Johnson cleared his throat. He swallowed hard while looking at a young dude who had barely lived life yet.

"Your babymother, she's been murdered."

As soon as the words left the detective's lips, Champ snapped and took off toward the house at the same time GG's body was being brought out of the house. More police officers jumped on Champ to hold him down on the detective's command. His heart was broken. He was shattered. His world had just crashed down in his face.

***

Brad and his partner landed in Atlanta. The agents were headed to the homicide unit downtown to pull files on Diamond's murder case. Brad wasn't surprise to see Pimp wiggled out of the case. He was a very slick person whom Brad wanted to put next to his even slicker dad.

When both FBI agents walked into the building, they commanded a sense of respect. Everyone stopped what they were doing as the men strolled straight into the captain's office.

The captain was an old white man with gray hair showing his age. He looked like one of them hunting-type, fishing-type white men with a hard look like he never smiled for no reason at all.

Brad closed the door behind him and his partner, then introduced himself.

"Special Agent Brad. I need files pulled for the case of the pregnant woman, ASAP. Every report, every written statement, and especially the tapes," Brad said.

"That case was closed. Her murderer was murdered the same or next day," the captain said.

"Just grab them files, captain," Brad demanded.

"If you say so." The captain motioned for one of the many detectives looking into his office. A female walked in.

"Yes, Cap?"

"Grab all the files on the Diamond Lewis case. Give them to these gentlemen after making copies," the captain told her.

"Yes, sir." The woman left to do as told. Brad took the time to ask the captain a few questions about Pimp and his history in Atlanta, if he had any.

"So, Captain, this Savarous Jones. Tell me something about him that you know." Brad and his partner took seats.

Never taking his eyes off both agents, the captain replied while sitting up, leaning over his desk.

"He's smart is what I can tell you. I know that much, but in these files you will not find Savarous. He's never been a problem in Atlanta at all."

"Sounds like you and Jones are on a personal level. Are you?" Brad asked.

"Look, sir, Mister Big Shot, I wanna catch Jones, too. But law is law, so we do what it takes." The captain was getting upset with the federal pressure he was getting.

Brad's partner smiled, and so did Brad.

"Just get what I need, Cap."

***

Pimp made a phone call to Yolanda from a burner cell phone. He was parked in a Walmart parking lot, waiting on Donte to come pick him up. Yolanda picked up on the third ring.

"Hello?"

"Wassup, babygirl?"

"You probably need to get a lawyer. Feds asking questions. They mentioned Diamond name, Honey and Donte. And we need to talk face-to-face 'cause I got a bone to pick with you, for real, for real," Yolanda said.

"Ok, cool. How you doing, though?" Pimp asked, changing the subject. He had heard enough already, so his next move had to be before the feds' strike.

"I'm ok, but 'how are you' is the question. Don't you

think you should slow down, or better yet just stop?"

She was talking crazy again. He had to get off the phone with her ass. "Listen, I'll see you in a few days. Don't make plans."

Pimp didn't give her a chance to reply. He just hung up the phone and got back into the low-key car he was riding around in. Moments later, Donte pulled up in Pimp's Benz, driving solo. Pimp wasted not a second jumping out of the Honda he was driving.

He had with him the kilo of dope and the cellphone in a bag. He jumped in the passenger side and dapped Donte as the Benz pulled off.

"What's up, big homie? You good?" Donte asked.

"Hell yeah, just got a phone call from Yolanda. She said the feds asking 'bout me and the team. Yo' name came up, too, but these hos ain't talking 'bout shit. We clean. We can't do nothing 'bout them looking, though," Pimp replied and got a shake of the head from Donte, agreeing then he added, "Did Montay find out who this nigga is riding around bulletproof?"

"I'on even know, big homie," Donte shot back.

"Okay, take me to the condo. He should be there or the club."

"Why don't you call 'im"

"I'm not fucking with these phones for awhile. Stay offline, too, my nigga, especially since the feds got they weak-ass press game down," Pimp told his partner while they headed to the condo.

"Good thinking, big homie. So, you say the feds way up in the north asking 'bout us? Do you know exactly what they could have on us?" Donte wanted to make sure Pimp had everything airtight.

"To be honest, I think they flexing. But you can never

be too sure with federal, so I got lawyers on our team. You got nothing to worry about, my nigga. I crossed all T's and dot all I's," Pimp assured Donte, and moments later they pulled up at the condo.

Montay was there with Donte's shooter. Both were counting up money and smoking when Pimp walked in, followed by Donte.

"What's up, boy? I'm glad you showed up. I got some info for you," Montay said and tossed the money he had in his hand on the table. He stood up, then grabbed a bottle of water that sat on the table. He and Pimp walked over to the kitchen counter.

"What's the info?" Pimp asked. He needed good news right then.

"The niggas that got murked the other day that we thought was those Pine Street boys? Come to find out the niggas was paid to snatch you up. The motherfucker behind this is Devil. His babyma name is Taylor. Do that name ring bells?" Montay gave him that look like Pimp slipped somewhere down the line.

"Yeah. Oh, so this nigga in his feeling? Do you got any whereabouts, this nigga home address, or any of that?" Since he wanted to beef, Pimp would bring it to him.

"Yeah, I got all that. The nigga owns half Miami. He's plugged in with cops an' all, plus he got the network. Getting this nigga gonna prove to be hard as a mothafucka 'cause he ride bulletproof, then his security deep," Montay said.

Pimp nodded his agreement to what he just said, then he spoke. "I gotta let him come to me, then."

"Exactly."

"Yeah, that's the move. So listen, we gonna close

everything down we doing except the sports bar. I gotta focus solely on this nigga, and at the same time watch the feds 'cause they on my ass hard."

"I'm witcha."

Pimp walked over to where Donte was. He told him about closing every operation they had going so they could catch this bulletproof-riding-ass nigga. Donte was down with the plan as he was down for every plan, so it was settled. Their focus was going to this dude, Big Guy.

Chapter Seven

The Devil in Me

Devil sat like a king inside his Maybach, talking business on his cellphone like always. Cake sat next to him, Drako laid across her lap, looking left to right as they rode down through Pokey Bean Project, hoping they could run into Pimp.

Walking down the street was a group of boys and girls who Big Guy decided to ask a few questions, so he made his driver stop.

"Pull up on those kids," he spoke over his phone call, tapping the headrest of the driver's seat and pointing in the direction in he was speaking.

The driver did as told and swerved to the side. The two SUVs also pulled up to the side. Devil rolled his window down. "Hey, come here. Any one of you."

Ashley and Cindy were among the group, but neither were the kid to walk over to the Benz. Only a younger dude knew who Big Guy was when he saw him. He was the one who stepped over to the half-cracked window.

"Wassup?"

"What's going on around here, young blood?" Devil asked.

"What you mean, homie?" the young dude was curious.

"Why is the block so dead?"

"Oh, it's hot 'round here. Them out-of-town dudes got the police everywhere."

"Out of town? Who, Pimp 'n them?" asked Devil and got the answer he was looking for.

"Yeah, and his crew."

"Have you seen 'im?"

"Nawl, but they," the boy pointed to the girls, "know him."

"Oh yeah?" Devil looked at the girls.

"Yeah. Aye, Cindy, c'mere," the young kid called one of the girls over, but both came with no hesitation.

Devil judged neither to be eighteen years old. He put on his best smile as they approached the Benz.

"What?" Cindy said, then looked into the Benz to Devil and Cake, then back to the boy.

"Big homie wanted to holla atcha," the boy said.

"What's up?" Cindy asked, looking into the Benz again.

"Pretty self, I'm looking for Pimp and I heard you can help me. And for anyone who helps me, I make sure they are well paid. I don't know if you know who I am, but I run this city. My name holds weight 'round here," Devil told her. Any lil' young female would jump all over that offer. Broke, busted, and disgusted, a few hundred would put her pockets where they needed to be.

"I don't mess with Pimp like that. He got a sports bar, that's 'bout all I kn –" she lied.

"He got a condo downtown," Ashley blurted out. Cindy hit her arm in a slick manner that she tried to hide from Devil, but he peeped it.

"Downtown. Okay. And what's yo' name?" Devil turned his focus on Ashley.

"We gotta go." Cindy snatched her friend away from the Benz because she was talking too much.

Devil rolled the window back up and said to Cake, "Have both them lil' bitches picked up." The Maybach pulled off, leaving the projects.

"I'm on it," Cake wickedly smiled a sexy smirk and

text someone in one of the SUVs with them.

"I believe this nigga done went into hiding or something. Pussy-nigga gon' get what's coming to 'im," Devil said.

"And I can't wait, baby," replied Cake and meant it.

A few hours later, after he sent a carload of gunners to Pimp's sports bar, Devil retired to his duck-off. Going to the club was a no-no for him, plus he had important business to handle. It pissed him off Pimp wasn't found thus far, so he upped the price on Pimp's head, dead or alive. Fuck it.

He had ten niggas looking to kill Pimp when spotted, so now he could just relax and await the phone call. Cake was in the shower while Devil sat at the laptop going over business contracts. His cell phone rang, showing his wife calling. Removing his glasses and leaning up to grab his phone, Devil answered.

"Yes, love"

"Baby, Kristy is sick. Very, very sick. I'm about to take her to the doctor. She's running a fever of 107. She hasn't eaten or anything of that nature." Kristy was his youngest daughter.

"What caused this? Are you taking her or calling –"

"I want us to take her," his wife cut him off.

He heard in her voice that she needed him. Without hesitation, Devil said, "I'm on the way, love."

"Okay, baby. We're waiting on you," his wife replied. She sounded hopeful, and that's what Devil liked.

Closing the laptop, he stood up, preparing to leave. He called his driver, then walked into the bathroom to put Cake on point.

***

Every idea Brad had, Pimp had already sealed air tight. He was steps ahead of the government, but Brad wasn't fooled. He knew Pimp was everything Icey thought he wasn't. All Brad wanted was the chance to prove to Icey he was right.

Brad wasn't able to get much info on Pimp in his hometown, and no info at all in Texas. But he did run another one of Pimp's girls down. Her name was Honey, and she offered up no help at all.

Brad's head was hurting. He wanted to give up, but at the same time he knew Icey was in danger. He had to save his childhood friend's life, whether she liked it or not, and he knew she wasn't gonna like this.

Icey was head-over-heels with Pimp, and Brad hated it. She was so in love with this man that she was blind. Brad knew his best friend to be this soft-spoken, caring, and smart girl. Since they'd been best friends, he'd never witnessed her in a relationship with a thug. Icey always dated well-respected men with good backgrounds.

She was in big trouble if she kept the kid she was pregnant with. She would also go down in Pimp's crime, and Brad could not sit and see that day.

It was a windy morning in New York as Brad and his partner walked into a clothing store. The girl they were looking for worked there. She was helping a customer when the agents entered the store. She didn't look up from what she was doing, so she didn't notice them as they waited and watched her.

This woman was the last person they had to question about Pimp, and from the things they've heard about her, she was the best help they could get.

Another ten minutes passed, then finally she was free. That's when Brad leapt into action, pulling his ID out and showing her before saying, "FBI. I need to have a few words with you, ma'am."

Honey wasn't shocked to see them, but she was surprised they found her when she left North Carolina. She thought she left her part there, also. She had a new life, a good life she has started with her daughter and boyfriend. She did not need any problems right now.

Honey swallowed hard, but refused to let the FBI see her shook. She put on a fake smile and said, "Okay, how can I help you?"

Brad pulled out that same photo of Pimp and gave it to her. Honey took the picture and looked at it a moment, then passed it back.

"You know him, right?"

"Yes, that's Pimp," she answered quickly.

"And what's your relationship with –"

"Friendship," she corrected him.

"Well, from what I've learned, you were his top girl. I'm not coming here to put you in jail, to bash you, or to stir up your new life. I came here asking for your help by giving me the info I need on Savarous Jones," Brad said as calmly as possible.

"And how can I do that? What info?"

"Just tell me some things about Pimp we maybe don't. Know anything helpful?"

"Sir, I cannot help you with that. All I know about Pimp is that he's a good person, very sensitive, passionate, and humble. Pimp really don't get into much," she lied, and they knew it.

"Really? You gonna play me out like that?" the agent asked her, clearly offended.

"I'm not playing you at all. I'm being honest." Honey smiled, then excused herself to get back to work. "Excuse me, sir."

"Okay, smart ass. Let's just say I'm federal government that can dig into any past I want. Pray hard I find no dirt." Brad was heated as Honey kept walking, acting as if she didn't hear him. They were running out of options. Brad and his partner left the clothing store empty-handed with no information and a great big waste of money spent on hotels, gas and food.

On their way back to the airport, Brad made a promise to himself to put Pimp behind bars. Nothing would stop nor slow him down at all. He wanted Pimp so bad he could taste him. He could smell victory over Savarous Jones, and that's what he was after: victory.

***

Devil and his driver pulled up to his beautiful home, a white brick house trimmed in red wood. Its stunning brick driveway and healthy green grass also set the home off. He had cameras everywhere, and it was gated with a code and heavy security at the front.

Devil's Maybach automatically opened the gates. His wife's Benz also did this, but everyone else needed codes.

His driver parked the Benz in its spot and Devil got out. It felt good being home and away from the drama the streets brought. He was more worried about his daughter's sickness than anything, so he walked into his plushed crib.

Devil closed the door and saw no sign of his wife, their dog, or daughter. He walked into the kitchen, then decided to call her name out loud.

"Misty? Baby, I'm home," his voice carried through the big house as he walked upstairs, headed to the rooms. It was quiet, unlike the house he knew.

It was strange 'cause there were no cooks, no cleaner, no kids. Devil wondered if his wife went ahead and took Kristy to the hospital. Was she that sick?

When Devil walked into the master bedroom, his heart dropped to the pit of his stomach. Nothing in the world could make him believe Pimp had the upper hand. What he saw had to be a dream. It just couldn't be that Pimp was sitting next to his tied-up wife and kids.

Devil was a smart man, and also a long thinker. He was the type to almost always talk himself out of situations. He knew this was the time, if any, to start talking and not try any hero shit.

"Hold what you got, young blood." Devil held both hands up, pleading for time. Pimp stood to his feet. Donte was in a corner of the room holding a choppa.

"Nawl, pussy-nigga, you hold what the fuck you got. Where is that cash stash at? I know you got one," Pimp said.

"I got cash," Devil said, hoping it would buy him some time.

"Where is it?"

"My safe. Listen, young blood, just let my kids and wife go and do whatever you want with me," said Devil.

"Shut the fuck up, nigga! Fuck, you thought it was gon' be sweet or something?"

"Nawl. Nawl, I didn't think it was sweet, brother. I was just looking for some form of understanding. Why did you take Taylor out when she was a wonderful mother, good person at heart?" Devil asked the question he planned on asking Pimp once he had him caught and at his mercy, but it was Pimp who had the upper hand.

"Taylor?"

"Yeah, the female you killed on 63rd."

"You must be the cops? How da fuck you figure I was the one who murdered the ho? You believe everything you hear?" Pimp shot back.

"I don't know what to believe, young blood, but now I'm asking you yourself. Did you take her out?"

"Take me to that safe, I'll tell you," Pimp replied.

Hesitant to move, Devil finally led Pimp to an office room where he tried again to talk to Pimp. He tried to talk his way out of this mess. "Young blood, I got three hundred and fifty cash. It's yours, just spare my life, homie. I'm a OG in the game. I got kids near yo' age. I just want to live my life."

"Nigga, show me that safe. Stop motherfucking begging like a bitch. You 6'9", nigga. I'm 5'7", and you still ain't tried nothing. No wonder you ride around in a bulletproof car." Pimp pointed the gun directly at the bigger dude's face, ready to dead him.

"I'm not trying you 'cause it's not what you think."

"If I say one mo' word 'bout that safe –"

"Okay, okay. Over here," Devil pointed behind the desk and walked over. Pimp followed him, and that's when Devil thought he could get away with pulling a stunt. He turned and tried to kick Pimp, but failed. What he did kick was the gun, nearly knocking it out of Pimp's hand.

Pimp lost his balance briefly. Devil could've had him, but he was scared already, so he went for the gun he kept under the desk. Pimp, on the other hand, stumbled back, but his grip was tight on the gun. He knew Devil was only trying to get space.

Pimp caught his balance. He aimed at the top of Devil's back and neck. He let off four shots.

Boom, boom, boom, boom.

Bullets tore out of the front of Devil's face, instantly killing him. More shots rang out upstairs. Pimp already knew by the number of shots that Donte handled his business.

He and Donte met at the front door, no words spoken. What was understood didn't have to be explained. They walked out of the house just as they came in, mission completed.

Jerry Jackson

Chapter Eight

Love Me without Mercy

It was another night Pimp came home late and horny. For the past few days it'd been his routine to come home late, get in the shower, and then fuck her good until they both fell asleep.

He had been in the streets heavy since everything was in the open. Tonight was a different night, though. It was him telling her, "Icey, I don't know what it is about you, but you got me so in love with yo' ass. I'm crazy 'bout you, no lie. Listen, baby, I want and need you to move with me to Atlanta. It's a new start for me. It's a good place to start, and I wouldn't do it without you. Please stop everything and move with me to Atlanta."

Icey was hush-mouthed for a moment after Pimp spoke those words. All she could do was look at him in the darkness. She was in love like he was, too, and she was happy with their situation. But at the same time she did not want to just give up her dreams and goals. She did not want to give up on the kids who depended on her at the art school. Pimp was her life, also, and their baby was their future together, so this was a choice she was forced to make. Icey cleared her throat and stared at the man she wanted forever with.

"Savarous, I'll do anything for you. All I ask is that you do not put me in a situation. I will remain in business here, though, because I cannot let my school down, nor will I stop teaching from time to time. Anything else I'll do, baby," she said.

Pimp smiled 'cause her news made him happy. It was what he wanted to hear. "That's what's up, baby. I got you," Pimp replied and they kissed. Icey was as happy as she could be. She didn't think Pimp was as bad as it seemed.

She didn't realize he had just murdered a family in cold blood, and then came and made love to her like it was nothing. She didn't expect it to be like it really was, but it was.

Pimp pulled her into his arms more. She was so soft and smelled so beautifully good. It just felt great to cuddle.

After they broke their kiss, Pimp slid down her body so he faced her belly. He kissed her stomach and rubbed her.

Icey rubbed his head and thanked God for this man. "I love you so much, I swear," she mumbled.

Pimp came back up face-to-face with her. He kissed her once more. "I love you more, baby girl."

The second time they made love was one of their best sessions. Icey took her time feeling every part of Pimp there was to feel. They kissed through nearly every position, and every position they stayed in at least five minutes.

Pimp had one of her legs tossed over his shoulder. Her other leg was open as well, but her feet braced his shoulder while her hand rested on his stomach, keeping him at bay. Pimp had sweat dripping down his naked body as he slowly made love to his woman.

Icey accepted every stroke as a feeling of love. Her pussy was so wet as his hardness filled her up. Pimp went deep into Icey's warm love. It hurt, but it felt 100% better, especially since she was in love with this man.

Icey's body tensed up from the amazing sensation she was feeling when he took her there. Her pussy muscles gripped his dick. She wrapped her arms around him tight and bit into his shoulder softly.

Pimp kept grinding into her, but not too hard. He took his time because he knew she was pregnant and he didn't want to hurt the baby.

Pimp slowed his pace to just good lovemaking after she came for a second time. He kissed her deep and slowly went in and out of her wetness. He did circular motions every so often, going deep.

They sucked each other's tongues and moaned into one another's mouths.

Icey's eyes were closed, and she was silently thanking God for Savarous Jones. Pimp's eyes were opened looking at the woman he loved and wanted to truly be with.

Pimp hugged her and started grinding a lil' harder, a lil' deeper. Icey had to tighten her thighs a bit to keep him from going crazy inside her. He caught the hint and just met his mark when he came inside her, at the same time kissing her.

It was still early, so sleep found them again. They held each other as the sun peeked through the blinds. Icey didn't pay no attention to her ringing phone. Neither did Pimp to his own.

All they could think about was the love they were feeling, a love that had them both hooked.

***

News hit the streets of Miami fast that Big Guy and his family were murdered. The talk was a mob hit because didn't nobody think two hood niggas pulled this stunt. Nobody but Cake.

She was crushed by the news and swiftly plotted some get-back on Pimp and his operation. No matter how much it cost, no matter how hard it seemed, Cake vowed to make it happen. First things first, she sent some shooters over to Pimp's sports bar to shoot it up. This was just a warning shot, a message she knew Pimp was behind this.

It did bother Cake how Big Guy slipped. She knew her own mistake was made because her gut told her something was not right. She should have said something when he told her he was going home. She should've told him how she felt.

Tears approached her eyes. As soft as she looked, as cute as she was, anyone would think she would break. Cake thought she was gangsta, so she wouldn't let a tear fall.

She wiped her eyes, then grabbed her Drako. Cake had so much shit to take care of. Big Guy had a lot of business in Miami on a high level and more dirty business in the underground world.

Cake knew the whole operation on the dirt, but as far as business she had no clue. The whole crew was lost. Everyone was baffled because Big Guy was the plugg. Big Guy was the way everyone ate. Cake called a meeting at one of Big Guy's wearhouses she had access to. It was later that night, so as of now she would go secure what cash she could of Big Guy's.

Ridig solo in the bulletproof Benz, Cake got a call she wasn't expecting, but one that gave her a change of plan.

"Hello," she answered.

"Cake, wassup ma? This Blue Eye. I got some intel on that nigga, Pimp." Blue Eye was one of Big Guy's loyal money men. He was the typical guy who sold information at a high price.

"Okay, shoot," Cake said.

"Icey Williams. She's an art student or teacher. He's in love with her. You get to her, you get to him."

"Good. I need address and full name, and I'll see you in a few days." Cake was happy with this news.

"I'm sending it over now," Blue Eye replied.

A smile crept to her face as she thought about how Pimp would look when he was caught off guard. Icey Williams had to get it no matter who she was because if Pimp loved her, then Cake would destroy her without mercy.

***

The first place she stopped by was Devil's main spot in downtown Miami. The condo was where he kept a load of cash and drugs. Not too many people knew about this spot.

When Cake got there, she used the key to unlock the safe hidden in the bottom of the closet.

Cake got the surprise of her life when she saw more cash than expected. The safe was packed full with colorful money.

She pulled her cell phone out. She had to move the money to a different spot, one everyone didn't know of. Cake took a seat on the edge of the bed, the phone to her ear, waiting on one of Devil's money movers to pick up.

"Yo."

His name was Smith. He'd been with Devil ten years, driving money from point A to point B. He was the one Devil always called on the important moves.

"Hey, I need you at the condo, like, ASAP," Cake said into the phone.

"Okay, I'm en route." There were no questions asked. Smith had always been Devil's first choice, and now Cake saw why.

She relaxed on the bed, looking at all the money in the safe.

"Bae wasn't playing," she said to herself and knew it would be a great task filling his shoes.

***

At first he thought he was dreaming when Icey kept pushing him to wake up. He was tired and didn't even wanna open his eyes. All Pimp wanted was thirty more minutes to rest, but Icey wouldn't give up.

"Baby, get up. I think something is wrong." She pushed his arm and shook him.

"With the baby?" Pimp asked in a crack, tired voice.

"No, your phone nonstop ringing." Icey grabbed it, then gave it to him. As soon as Pimp had it in his hand, it started ringing again, and without looking at the screen he picked up.

"Yeah."

"We got a problem, bruh. Get up. Meet me at the club." It was Montay.

"A problem?" Pimp sat up with that question. He was fully woke now. His mind was at full attention.

"Motherfuckas done shot the club up. Just got a call from Donte saying detectives riding around with his picture, too," Montay said. Pimp began to get to his feet as his mind clicked on what move to make. Icey also got up with a sudden worried look to her face. She didn't say anything, just looked, and she didn't have to say nothing because Pimp saw it in her face.

"Did anyone get hurt?"

"Unfortunately, yes. I got the cops here, also," Montay replied.

"Okay, is it bad?"

"Nothing insurance can't handle."

"Alright, I'm 'bout to leave now, then. Give me a minute," Pimp said.

"Baby, what's going on?" Icey decided to ask as she watched Pimp get ready to leave. She instantly got worried, not knowing what to think.

Pimp looked at her and told her the truth. "Club got shot up. I'm just 'bout to meet my business partner there, that's all, baby girl."

"I have a question, baby." Icey got up out of the bed. Pimp was putting on his shoes.

"Wassup?"

"Do this have anything to do with you? I mean, like, is anyone trying to kill you or anything like that?"

When she asked that question, Pimp stopped what he was doing. He walked over to his woman. Icey felt safe when he was close to her. He pulled her into his arms and kissed the top of her head.

"Heck nawl, baby. That's probably some young lil' dudes acting their age. You don't have anything to worry about, okay?" Pimp had to reassure her.

"Okay, baby," Icey said back and hugged him tight. "So, can I roll with you?" she added and looked up to his sexy face.

Pimp gave it a quick thought. He had already lied to her about the shooting, and now she wanted to hang. The police would be there, so he wasn't worried about niggas trying something, but he still didn't want his girl with him. Beef was all in the streets, and right then anything went. He didn't want to tell her no, but he didn't want to say yes, either.

Again, he kissed her and said, "I see you not gonna take my 'no', being that you getting dressed. But after I hit this club, I'ma drop you off, okay?"

"Huh? Okay," she smiled. She was happy.

***

Brad was drained from so much ground work, airplane rides, and stubborn people. He was back in Miami and had to go back lowkey due to him being suspended.

Since being in Miami, he'd been calling and texting Icey and got not one response back. Even when they were really, really mad at each other, even when they felt they hated each other, they had never ignored their code. Brad had sent the code at least ten times since first calling and texting last night on the plane ride. He was worried because this was unlike Icey, and what panicked him more was when he called her mother and explained what was going on, she hadn't heard from Icey, either.

"So, Brad, tell me what's with this Savarous guy?" Icey's mother had asked him. All she knew of Pimp was what Icey had told her, and that was everything good. Mrs. Williams had no idea her daughter was dealing with a guy who was number one on all of the federal government lists.

"Well, like I've told you, this boyfriend of Icey is a known drug pusher and a killer who is slick enough to get past the FBI. He has somehow brainwashed Icey into thinking he was this prince charming dude. I have did everything to show her his true color. I have bent over backwards for Icey, and guess what?" Brad didn't wait. "She told him I was tracking him under the rug. This situation almost cost me my job. She told me we wasn't friends anymore and she chose him over me." Brad was pissed.

"Oh, my God. Lord have mercy," were the only words that came out of Icey's mother's lips. All this time she thought her daughter was with this perfect guy.

"I know."

"I'm about to call her. Have you been to her place?" Mrs. Williams wanted to know.

"I'm headed there now," replied Brad.

"Okay. I'll also call the school and shop. When I hear from her, I'll call and let you know what's going on."

Brad agreed and moments later he hung up the phone.

Icey was gonna really hate him now that he'd told her mother the truth about who Pimp was. He didn't know what else to do. He was all out of options, and all he wanted was his friend safe.

Tired, Brad drove the busy streets of Miami, he pulled over at a local gas station to grab him a Red Bull and some chips. Brad parked and got out in front of the store. On the side of him was a car full of teenage boys and one girl driver. Brad really didn't pay them no mind as he headed into the store.

Walking in, another teen walked out talking trash to the guy inside the store. The teen boy had a mouthful of gold teeth. Brad entered the store and found his items, then paid for them.

Just one more week, thought Brad, and he would be back to work. He promised to build a case on Pimp that he couldn't beat. It didn't matter if he cheated doing so. He was willing to bend whatever rule he had to bend.

Pimp came out of the blue skies and stole his one and only true friend. Brad couldn't let that happen.

It was almost 11:00 a.m. when Brad made it to Icey and Pimp's home. He felt funny pulling up there since it was his first time there, but he would do anything to save his friend.

When Brad pulled up on the block, he noticed the same car from the gas station that had the kids in it. This time it was empty 'cept the girl, and that made Brad get on alert as he slowly rode past the car. He didn't pull into the driveway.

Icey could be in danger. Brad knew he had to take action right then and there. He parked the car down out of sight and jumped out with his gun in hand, he could only remember seeing three guys in the car at the gas station.

Icey and Pimp shared a house surrounded by gates and big bushes, which made it hard to see the house from the outside. Those same bushes helped hide him, also, as he crept up toward the car, gun ready to blast if need be. All he could think about was someone hurting Icey because of Pimp's actions in the streets.

The closer Brad got to the girl in the car, the nervousness got greater. He didn't know what to expect, what to think.

The girl inside the car was a young girl who probably didn't know what was going on, probably was just driving for her boyfriend or something. Brad jumped out on her, gun aimed and badge hanging around his neck.

"Don't move. Put yo' hands, both hands, on the steering wheel. FBI," Brad demanded.

The young girl jumped. She had a shocked look on her baby face and tears formed in her eyes. She did as told and broke down crying like she knew she was in big trouble not just with the law, but with her parents. She broke down crying just like a lil' kid.

Brad snatched the door open. He roughly pulled her out to the ground. He couldn't play with her right then, so he quickly placed the cuffs on her. He was bent down, hidden behind the car.

"Sir, please!"

"How many people you're with?" Brad's first question came.

"Four. I'm just driving, but I do not know what's going on, sir. I promise," the girl answered through tears.

"How many guns they have? What are they doing?"

"I don't know, I swear!"

"You going down with them, then," Brad said. He quickly opened his phone and called his boss.

"I swear to God, sir, I just saw, like, two guns. I don't know! I swear I don't, sir," she cried harder.

Brad heard the phone ring a few times, then his boss picked up.

"Brad, what's up? I'm in a meeting."

"Sir, I have a situation. I know I'm not active, but I was out here at my best friend's house and just rode up on a driver outside her home and three guys inside she said has guns. I have her detained, but I did not want to proceed without your sign off, nor without some backup," Brad told his boss while watching for any of the boys to round the corner.

"What's going on over there that has people outside her home? I'm sending a team to your location. When they get there, you stand down," his boss stated, which made Brad dislike him even more.

Brad didn't let him know, though. He just said back, "Yes, sir, will do."

Jerry Jackson

Chapter Nine

Still In the Midst of This Beef

When Pimp and Icey got to the sports bar, it was a total mess out there. Montay was standing out front talking to the cops. He had a dismayed look upon his face.

Pimp saw the bullet-ridden building with nearly all of the glass shot out, crime scene tape covering the entire area as police officers did their investigation. He wanted to know who was behind this shooting. He knew he had knocked the buck out of them Pine Street dudes, so it couldn't be them. Or could it?

Pimp parked and leaned over to his girl. He kissed Icey's lips softly before saying, "I'll be right back, baby girl"

"Alright, boo," Icey said as she watched him get out and walk over to where Montay stood.

Pimp walked over and shook both Montay and the officer's hands. He has to carry himself as professionally as possible to play his role.

"Savarous, this is Detective Murray. Murray, this is my partner, co-owner of the sports bar," Montay introduced them.

"Okay, what's going on?" Pimp asked the policeman, who had a pen and pad in hand, writing something down.

The detective read from the pad. "As it stands, we only have two suspects in custody and nobody hurt. Nothing else major except the building."

"So, no one was hurt?" asked Pimp, then looked at the building. He wanted to know who the two suspects were.

"Lucky. Blessed, I know," Detective Murray replied with a slight chuckle.

"Shit, that's good. I know insurance will handle the damages," Pimp cut back in. He took Montay by the shoulder and excused them from the cop.

They both walked off to talk, but neither noticed Champ and Mel walking up the block.

***

"That's them niggas right there, bruh," Mel said to Champ after they decided to get out of their ride and walk over to the sports bar.

All Champ had in his mind was murder, but when he and Mel had pulled up, they noticed police were everywhere and wondered what happened, hoping Pimp was one of the people who got murdered 'cause from where they were parked, it looked just like a murder case.

Champ tucked his gun and Mel followed suit, they both stood across the street from the club and watched Pimp and one of his partners interact with a cop.

Champ's blood boiled hot as thoughts of his girlfriend, GG, and what Pimp did to her surfaced in his mind. He was hurt most of all behind the loss of his unborn and GG's lives. He felt sorry for his step-daughter losing her mom.

He vowed to catch and kill Pimp, but he wasn't gonna go about it stupid and in his feelings.

As for Mel, he really didn't give a fuck.

"Let's just go blasting them fuck-niggas." Mel was emotional and didn't care like he usually did.

"Nawl, we gonna follow these niggas when they leave, cuz. We don't need to be on the news for killing them and the police," Champ told his cousin and kept a watchful eye on Pimp. See, this nigga Pimp had somehow murdered both their girlfriends and their cousin Tuck. There was no getting away. It was payback time, but Champ wanted to do it right, surprisingly, and Mel didn't care.

"Man, these folks gonna be out here all day and night, and I don't got time to be trying to follow these niggas. All I'ma do is catch the car at the next light and blast they ass." Mel gripped the gun hidden under his shirt.

"That's good, too, but I want these niggas dead, not just shot the fuck up. I want these niggas just as bad as you do, but I'm not trying to be in jail. I got shit to take care of, my nigga, for real," Champ tried to calm his cousin.

Mel could only shake his head while still watching Pimp and his friend walk away from the cop. Pimp had killed his brother. "Yeah, I hear you, cuz. But look, these niggas walking off. I'm 'bout to just run up, my nigga. Fuck dat."

Mel pulled out his gun. Champ grabbed him, but Mel shook away. "Nawl, watch out." Mel headed toward them after getting out of the car.

***

Icey got a text from Brad while she sat waiting on Pimp to return. She watched him talk to the police and then walk off with Montay. Her love for Pimp was the only thing that had her with him, and the fact she was walking around with his seed.

Her phone had three missed calls and two text messges, all from Brad. She opened the message even though he was the last person she wanted to talk to. She knew something had to be wrong.

Call me ASAP something has happened at your house, the text read.

Icey shook her head, then looked up from her phone to see two dudes across the street from her. Both guys were looking at Pimp. Something had told her to look up, and she was glad she did because she got to see one of the guys pull a gun out.

Icey nearly panicked when she saw the guy with the gun was coming toward them. She blew the horn to get Pimp's attention. *Honk! Honk!* She saw Pimp quickly turn.

He saw her point, then saw what she saw. Pimp had to think and take action when he saw Mel with his gun out and coming toward him and Montay. Pimp's strap was in the car and Montay didn't have his pistol. Neither guy thought Mel or Champ was jail-bound.

Pimp did the next best thing since the stupid nigga wanted to show off in front of the police: he called them.

"Hey, he got a gun! He got a gun!" Pimp and Montay both took off running toward the police, who also saw Mel.

Mel raised his glock and fired in the direction of Pimp and Montay, running down the street toward the club.

"Freeze! Police! Drop the –" The cops couldn't get it out quick enough 'cause Mel pulled the trigger.

Boom, boom, boom.

All the cops and detectives ducked and took cover, then after Pimp and Montay were out of the way of a clear shot, they all returned fire on Mel, chopping him down mid-stride.

Pimp laughed on the inside at the stupid nigga Mel, then noticed Champ jumping in a car and pulling off. He quickly got to his feet.

"Everyone okay?" one of the detectives asked.

Pimp was worried about his girl. He ran away from the car for a reason.

Icey was shaken by the dead body in the streets. "Baby, you straight?" Pimp got in and closed the door. A detective just opened his door back up. "Give me a second. I'm talking to my wife," Pimp said and closed the door back. "What's up?" he asked Icey.

"Savarous, baby, what's happening? I just wanna know, that's all, 'cause clearly that boy was 'bout to kill y'all."

Icey was scared. He could see it in her face, despite what she said about being okay.

"Baby, I promise to explain everything once we get home alone."

"Brad text saying something has happened at the house. He wanted me to call him," Icey cut him off.

"At our house?"

"Yes." Icey read the message again just to make sure it was correct.

"Well, call 'im. Put it on speaker, baby," Pimp replied. He wanted to know what the feds wanted this time.

"Alright, hold on." Icey did as asked by her man. Brad's line rang twice.

"Princess," he answered.

"What's going on, Brad? What happened?"

"Hey, you need to stay away from Savarous. There was people here at yo' house to kill him – or worse, you. We got three dudes and a girl in custody right now. Assault rifles and vests was found on them."

"Huh?"

"I'm at your house right now. Just locked up four

people on Savarous's property loaded with guns. Where are you so I can have you picked up? He's in great danger, and I do not want you to become caught up in his web," Brad told her, not knowing Pimp was also on the phone.

"Oh my God. Well, I'm with Savarous right now, Brad, and I see what's going on first-hand. Thank you for the information, though."

"Icey, listen to me –"

She hung up the phone and powered it off. She looked at Pimp and asked, "How true is any of this?"

"Baby, he flexing. And like I said, I'll explain everything later. Let me handle this shit with the cops right quick."

"I'm coming with you."

"Well, come on, then," Pimp said and got out of the Benz. She followed him and came around to hold his hand as he walked over to the detective.

***

Brad made it downtown to the federal building and met his boss at the elevator. Mr. Murray was a black man in his late fifties. He was a hard man and very direct. Brad knew he probably was in trouble, as always, but he knew he wasn't wrong this time. He only had a few more days of suspension, but knew he would still be walking on thin ice dealing with Mr. Murray.

"Brad, you did good to save that family, plus this gives us a better view into Savarous Jones. You being suspended is just the rules, but great job on having a keen eye for the bad guy."

Mr. Murray surprised him with that statement.

"Thanks, sir." Brad didn't know what else to say, but he did have some questions, so he waited until they got on the elevator before he spoke. "So, is this Savarous Jones case in full swing? I mean, because I have some great Intel on him and things he's into." Brad pressed sixth floor on the panel.

"Yes, it's a full top-to-bottom investigation," Mr. Murray replied.

His answer made Brad smile 'cause that was something he wanted to hear. "Okay, sir. I'd be honored if I could be a part of it," Brad tried his luck. It was either yes or no, but he needed to know now.

"No problem. Matter fact, I'm going to place you head over the investigation because I know your heart is in it. But do not force nothing. Don't cheat or do too much. Don't make this case no personal matter. This is a job, not a game."

Mr Murray surprised him greatly. He really didn't know how to take the news. "Great, sir. I will not let you down." Brad was excited by the news.

They got off on the floor where most agents had offices. Brad went into his office and pulled every file he had on Pimp. Whether Icey liked it or not, he was about to crash Pimp's car. He would get him off the streets for good.

Brad named the operation Best Friend. He vowed he would bring Pimp to justice. He would use every resource he had. All the pull and power he had, he was willing to use just to save his best friend.

Brad was happy to have lead on this case. He sat at his desk and bathed his mind in thoughts and ideas about what moves to make and what to stay away from. He just wasn't trying to mess up something that could be so, so good.

***

All she could think about was Pimp being dead and gone. Cake had all kind of tickets on his head. She was willing to spend her last on making sure Pimp was killed. Shooting the sports bar up was just a taste of the things to come. He hadn't seen nothing yet, him or his friends.

She had got the call that someone just attacked Pimp and the police, but Pimp still got away. This wasn't the news she wanted to hear at all. This news alone made her mad.

Cake drove the Benz slowly in thought, already missing the presence of Devil. She still couldn't believe he was gone. He was her everything, and Pimp took him away without giving him a chance to put up a fight. It just wasn't fair how it all happened. How did Devil slip up like he did and let this nigga inside his well-secured home? It was like Pimp was some ghost or something, how he moved.

Cake made up her mind that since it was hard to catch Pimp, she would go at the weakest link, which was Icey.

The crew she sent to go snatch up Icey was a failed mission. They made pure rookie mistakes, and she hated that fact. Feds had pick them up red-handed on the spot, so now Cake would pay Icey a visit herself.

After over an hour driving, she pulled the Benz up to Icey's art store with hopes the bitch was in there. Cake wiped the tears that found their way out of her eyes. She was still hurt by her king, her everything being murdered in his own home with his daughter and wife. It was just heartbreaking to know.

She took her pocket-size glock and put it on her hip as she got out of the car into the fresh Miami heat. She had to be strong. She had to hold shit down for her Devil, and every motherfucker who played a part in his death would get dealt with.

Cake didn't pay attention to the guy two cars down from her. She got out and so did he. She had her gun tucked and he had his gun out, but she still didn't see him 'cause she did not look around. She was so emotional she didn't notice him creep over toward her until it was too late.

Cake saw the dude, saw the flash of the gun's chrome features. She tried to reach for her own weapon, but the sound of gunfire erupted, and then the pain she felt in her stomach. Cake tried to run for cover, but the quicker, bigger dude was too much for her. His gun was powerful, knocking chunks out of her flesh when it hit her.

Cake got shot five times before she finally hit the ground. Life was leaving her body, and she wondered why this had to happen to her.

Cake saw him. She saw a face she'd seen before. She saw him point the gun. She saw the barrel. She saw the flame. But she felt nothing at all.

Boom!

***

Donte handled his business as planned by Pimp. Now he could leave Miami and chill in Atlanta for a minute before going back home. Right then the feds were lurking and he didn't wanna get caught up – or worse, locked up.

He left the parking lot of Icey's art store, now a murder crime scene. Donte pulled off and sent Pimp a message telling him the move. Donte had promise loyalty to Pimp years ago when they first met through his sister, Nevea, who Pimp used to date.

Pimp had always kept his words when it came to telling Donte something. Pimp had given him good game to walk with, and that's what Donte did. He stayed down with the money Pimp gave him and made a name for himself in the north. His whole team was eating and he couldn't wait to get back with them.

Donte was head of his family. Everyone depended on him. Pimp called and needed him, so he was there, but he was surely ready to get back home with his earnings.

It took Donte thirty minutes to make it to the condo. All he needed was his ID and money. He would leave everything else just to make a clean trip to Atlanta. Inside the condo, he went to the closet where his stash was. Nothing major was inside the condo but some guns and cash. Donte had nearly a million dollars cash money already since linking up with Pimp in Miami.

He quickly grabbed his gun when he heard something at the front door.

Nobody knew about this spot but Pimp and Montay. Donte knew they was at the club dealing with an issue, so who could this be at the door?

Donte put the bag of money down and gripped the gun tight, on alert for whatever beef came. He slowly crept toward the living room. When he got there, he saw the door knob was moving. Donte aimed at the door.

***

"Man, it's over with down here, bruh. This shit is crazy. It's not worth the money, my nigga, or nothing, not only is it niggas and the police, but now the feds bending every corner they can turn," Montay told Pimp as they walked and talked. There were more cops than ever now that there had been a murder. He and Pimp were just talking to detectives and cops about the attempt made on their life. Montay was tired of explaining to the police anything, let alone a murder or why it took place.

"I can dig it. I told you I'm out of here. You the one who wanted to keep this club, bruh," Pimp laughed a little.

"Well, fuck that. Fuck this club. Yo' ass need to come to my city and I'll show you how to triple them millions you got," Montay boasted, and Pimp knew what he was saying was real. But what Montay didn't know was Pimp was done in the dope game. Once he left Miami, his plan was to finish school and focus on his father because he'd gotten caught up in a drug dealer's life down in Miami, and now it was time to get on the right path and right mission.

"I'll be in the city, for sure, but I'll be on a different note," Pimp said, then looked over his shoulder for Icey, still waiting on him. "Let's wrap this shit up so we can go."

"Yeah, 'cause I'm tired as a motherfucker, bro, no lie. Wassup with Donte? He good?" Montay gave him a pound.

"Yeah, bruh, on his way to the city," replied Pimp.

"Well, shid, I'm 'bout to head out, too. I'll see you in a few, my nigga. And take care o' that beautiful girl you got," Montay added.

It was time to leave the club crime scene. The police were still out there thick. The news crew had come along with a big crowd of growing people. Pimp didn't want to keep his girl waiting, so he again gave Montay some dap.

"I'll catcha, bruh."

Pimp walked over to the car with Icey inside. Miami had been worse than Texas ever had been to Pimp. The only thing different was the money, Pimp thought.

When he sat in the plush leather seat of the Benz, he released a deep breath of air. Pimp cruck up while shaking his head.

"What, baby? Something else?" Icey asked, worried.

Pimp pulled off. "This wasn't my plan," replied Pimp, shaking his head. He pulled his F/N from under the seat and sat it across his lap. The gesture alone made Icey become nervous again as the Benz flashed up the streets.

"What was the plan from the get-go? What's going on, Savarous? You told me we will talk. You said you was gonna tell me what was going on," Icey tried to get the truth out of him. She wanted to understand what was going on and wanted to know how to stop it. Did he want it to stop? Where was his mindset? Icey was in love with someone she realized she really didn't know.

"I know I told you, and I haven't forgot. Just let me think one moment, baby, okay? You know if I tell you I got you, then I meant it."

Pimp checked his phone. His lawyer had text. He text him back while at the red light. Pimp had sent his lawyer to the house to check things out, and it was clear the feds had left. He also got the text from Donte sayin' he handled the business. Pimp had taken out everyone who thought they could take him out except Champ's bitch-ass. Pimp knew if he wanted to catch Champ, then he would have to stay in Miami a moment's time more than he cared for. He wanted to head out ASAP, meaning he probably had to spare the bitch-nigga Champ.

"Okay, baby. I believe in you," Icey said and meant it, which made Pimp love her even more for the love she gave him.

Jerry Jackson

Chapter Ten

WTF? Who the Hell? How Did This Happen?

Donte was ready to kill whoever for whatever beef he had, or beef Pimp had. Donte was about to face off with it. The only thing he was hoping was that it wasn't more than five niggas on the other side of the door. He didn't have enough bullets to take all them niggas out if it was five.

This thought alone made Donte take cover in the condo's hallway so if it was a lot of niggas, he could kill most of them before they killed him. His heart was beating wildly in his chest as he anticipated the threat that lurked on the other side of the door. Could it be this girl, Cake, had folks on him already? Did someone see him drive here? Was he followed?

It wasn't until he heard the sound of a police walkie talkie that he knew it was the cops. He heard the knob turn, then a loud bang. The door crashed open. Everything moved at a fast pace, but at the same time things moved slow as hell. The first thing Donte saw were the big letters "FBI" across a shield. Donte knew it was over with, said and done.

He knew to just drop the gun. Donte could not run because he was on the eighth floor, so he wouldn't make it out of the building. And he would not even consider the thought of jumping out of the window for no reason at all. The fall was too high. Donte knew he had to face these folks head-on, but do so being smart, and that was giving up without a fight.

"FBI! Search warrant! Search warrant! I got one! Don't move! Don't move! I got a gun! Don't move! FBI!"

Donte heard it all as he was being roughly cuffed up.

"Fuck!" yelled Donte, seeing his life just stop.

The federal agents snatched him up. He saw at least nine of them, and they were trashing the condo already. He shook his head when he thought about the million plus some in cash he would go down for, the drugs and guns, plus no telling what else the feds had on them.

Donte wanted to scream. His emotions were at a high point. He thought about his kids back home, his sister and mom, and everything he had going on back in life in Carolina.

Donte was hoping Pimp continued to keep his word and get his lawyers on it like he said he would. That was all the hope he had. He didn't have anything else going but hope.

"What's your name, son?" one of the FBI agents asked him.

"Donte Gibson. I need to see my lawyer! Don't ask me shit else," Donte said, and he meant it. The agent who asked him didn't do anything but smile at Donte while the other agents reported all the things they found. It was clear Donte was in big trouble.

**

When Pimp and Icey made it home, things didn't look out of place. They couldn't tell four people got arrested out there that day. Pimp pulled the Benz up behind the Range Rover and killed the engine. He reached over and took Icey's hand. They shared a look, not saying no words at all. Pimp's phone vibrated again twice, but he didn't check it. He and Icey released hands and got out. He left his phone in the console.

Inside their home, Pimp went straight to one of his maids to ask questions. Icey headed to their bedroom. Pimp found Mrs. Parks in her appointed bedroom. Mrs. Parks was very trustworthy and was the head maid of many more. She was also very humble and sweet as pie. Her husband also worked for Pimp. He was the one who kept the things around the house looking good and working good. Mrs. Parks was in her fifties and moved around good.

Pimp saw her looking at the TV when he walked into her room. "Mrs. Parks, did any of them agents come into the house?" Pimp asked her.

She looked up from the TV and smiled when she saw him, like always. "No, they didn't even knock," she replied.

"Did you get everything on tape?" He hoped she did.

"Yes, from the moment they pulled up. I even got the part when your girlfriend's best friend, the FBI guy, caught the driver. Some young little female."

"Okay, that's cool, then." He turned to leave. "I'll get it before I leave."

Pimp was glad for that information as he headed to his room, also. He knew now that he would have to answer all of Icey's questions. Everything she wanted to know, he knew he would answer.

She was sitting on the bed looking at her phone when he walked into the room. Icey looked up from reading the screen.

"Brad said two of the four people they caught over here was here to kidnap me. I'm only trying to figure out why, though. What do I have to do with any of this? Better yet, I thought this wasn't the life you was living," spoke Icey.

Pimp pondered first before he spoke. He wasn't trying to lose her with the truth about him. Yeah, she knew some of the things, but she really didn't know his get-down. "Baby, take off all of your clothes. Let's get in the water together so we can talk and I can explain everything to you first-hand," Pimp said. Right then he wasn't trusting nobody at all, not even himself.

Icey didn't argue with his demand; all she did was comply. Even through the hard times and bad moments, Icey still managed to captivate his eyes when she stripped down to her panties

Icey stepped into the water with him. Pimp sat first, and then she sat down between his legs. The water was warm to the touch. It felt great on her skin, on his tensed-up body. She felt his kiss to the back of her neck.

"I'm sorry, baby," Pimp said low in her ear.

When he spoke those words, it made her reach out and grab his hand. She placed Pimp's hand on her stomach before she said, "I'm just scared to lose you, Savarous, or you losing me. I just want to know everything will be okay, that we're gonna be okay."

Pimp kissed her behind the ear this time. He circled her stomach with light belly rubs. He was feeling the love he was hearing. He was loving the feeling he felt.

"I promise we both gonna be okay, baby. This is the reason I want us to leave here, so I can start fresh. I mean, I see and respect your life here, but I'm asking you to come start fresh with me. I'm not asking you to be a part of anything I got going on but my love, that's it," Pimp spoke his piece.

"So, answer me this, then, baby: what happened at the club?" Icey wanted to know.

"That shit at the club was some dumbass niggas

robbed and killed my friend. Now they are mad 'cause I've had both their babymas killed."

When Pimp said these words, he felt how Icey's body tensed up. She didn't speak one word. She didn't move for a moment, and that felt like forever.

"You wanted the truth, and I'm not trying to lie," Pimp added, which made her finally speak.

"Goodness, Savarous. So, is it over? What about the people that was sent to kidnap me? What's that about?"

"I handled that, too, baby. Trust me, you do not got anything to worry about anymore. That's unless you staying in Miami, meaning I'm staying if you do."

"What do you mean 'you handled it,' baby? Not when Brad got four people locked up for trying to kill me."

"I know that, baby, but the person who paid the money to make this happen is dead," Pimp assured her.

"Oh, my God, you had them killed, too?" Icey was shocked by his truth.

"Yes." Pimp was being honest whole-heartedly.

"Goodness, Savarous. Christ, baby, and what are you gonna do about the FBI? Brad said that it's an investigation on you. A full one," Icey added with concern.

"Baby, I'm not worried about yo' friend's police-ass." Pimp hated to hear his name, plain and simple. He wasn't thinking about the feds. He was about to deal with them once he left Miami, anyways. He wanted to tell Icey what she needed to hear and wanted to hear, but he couldn't. In the reality of things, Pimp was tired, and being truly in love made him see and realize different things.

He rubbed her belly some more. Icey placed her hand on top of his. "I'm just praying God fix this. Lord knows I love you, Savarous, and I'll die for you, but all I want is your safety, baby. I'm scared," Icey had to admit.

"Let's just leave, baby."

"When?"

"Now. Right now. Let's leave. I got us," Pimp said and meant it.

"Really, baby? For real, like, now?" Icey asked, turning to kinda look at him.

"On our child, I'm serious."

***

Brad was the first to interview Donte when he was arrested and brought in for questioning. He was excited a little, but also fearful. He knew arresting Donte could either make or break the case. He just didn't want Pimp to leave town once he found out Donte was booked.

Even before going into the room, Brad knew a lot already about Donte and his crew. They had well-paid lawyers and mostly everything was airtight, plus he was playing hardbody. The government was coming at him with their A-game, which was fact, and that's the same way Brad would continue.

When Brad and his partner Jimmy walked into the room with Donte, the young kid looked like a man-child in person. He was big, he was mean-looking, and the things the feds knew of him were deadly.

Brad, being street even though he was this white guy, he still had more street smarts than a lot of people around him. He walked in, snatched up a chair, and slammed it down next to a handcuffed Donte.

"You can keep playing hard if you want, but that shit ain't gonna get you nowhere. You making yourself look stupid while someone you care about don't give a fuck about you." Brad reached into his pocket and pulled out a folded paper. He opened it and read, "You've had two murder warrants down here two weeks. If he cared anything about you, don't you know you would've been out of Miami? But naw, he let you get caught at his condo with over a million dollars in cash, guns, and drugs. Sounds like a setup to me. And you up in here acting like you gonna keep it G-code?" Brad was pressing every button he could.

Donte looked at the FBI agent and wanted to laugh, but he just sat there like he's done twice before, this time making a third.

Donte was crushed on the inside, but he wouldn't let it show. Pimp had bricks in the condo he didn't know nothing about at all. He kinda felt like in some way, some fashion Pimp had played him for a sucka. Donte also knew the lawyers were working, so that's why he was chilling.

"Man, I need to see my lawyers. That mean I got more than one. That means I'm not giving a fuck what you think you got. You need to come on with the charges."

"Just the money and drugs will get you messed up alone. What you need to do is help yourself. All I want is a little information and I can make shit disappear," Brad pressed some more.

"Man, take me back to my mothafucking cell, homie. Stop playing wit' me, white boy."

"Oh, I got yo' white boy." Brad got up 'cause he knew there was nothing else to be done once Donte asked for his lawyer. It was his right. Brad would get him with paperwork, though. He would find something on Donte nobody could get off, the same as he would do Pimp.

Brad and Jimmy left the room, leaving it to someone

else to deal with. Brad didn't need Donte to get Pimp. Pimp was already caught up with small federal crimes. It was the big things that Brad needed proof on, but he still didn't need Donte.

He was also going hard about this case to prove to his best friend she was wrong about Savarous Jones. Brad was just trying to be her Superman 'cause he knew she was tripping. It was like this guy Pimp had slipped her a love bug or something she couldn't shake. As he's said many times before, he wouldn't let Pimp mess up her life.

His boss had called for a team sit-down. When Brad and Jimmy got to the room, it was packed full of a lot of agents and officers of the government. Everyone turned to look at the two partners walking into the room.

"Good you could make it," Mr. Murray spoke while standing up. Brad took his seat and so did Jimmy. On the screen of the TV was a big picture of Pimp and surrounding pictures of other people.

On the table in front of him Brad found a folder. He opened it to find a sheet of paper the exact same as the TV. He could see the pictures of everyone else, and his heart dropped when he saw a picture of Icey amongst them.

His boss started to talk. Brad was numb and his stomach had knots in it. He was going crazy on the inside. He badly wanted to say something, but didn't. He just listened to what Murray had to say.

"Savarous Jones is the suspect in a murder, traffi-cam, and tax evasion case. He's twenty-six years old from North Carolina. His father is serving life in the Atlanta Federal Camp. Savarous Jones graduated both high school and online college and now attends Clark in Atlanta, GA. He has a condo already, downtown, 17th floor, Room

1723 C. He also has a house recently built in Buckhead. The address is in your folders. Savarous Jones is a smart man who has figured a way around us, so let's be on point for this investigation 'cause right now all we got is the tax evasion on him, and that's nothing that will get him," Murray said, then pointed to a raised hand of one of the agents. "Yes?"

"Sir, is Jones planning to leave Miami for Atlanta?"

"I believe so. Listen, this is the first level of surveillance. All we are doing is following and putting together until we've got a case, so if he runs to Atlanta, then so are we. Him having a fresh start will have him in a comfort zone, an easy way in for us, so we play back. Brad is lead over the case. He will appoint and pick his twenty-man team. All of you have a rest period until Brad calls for a brief meeting. Any more questions?" Murray asked.

No one else said anything. Everyone just grabbed their folders and stood to leave the meeting. Brad was still in his feelings because his best friend was in the mix of Pimp bullshit and he warned her to fall back.

It really did something to him to know Icey could be in danger. Brad would try his best to keep her in the clear, but Icey would have to help herself.

Brad finally stood up to leave the room, also. Murray was still there, standing in his same spot as the room cleared out. Mr. Murray called,"Let me have a word with you, Brad"

Brad walked over even though he didn't wanna look at Murray right then. He tried his best to hide his emotions, but he couldn't, and that was the reason Murray called him over.

"What's going on, sir?" Brad asked.

"Clear her. I see the look on your face about Icey. I love her, too, but if she sleeps with the man, then she eats with him as well. I know Icey, and this is unlike her, but we still have a job to do. Follow by the rules," Murray said, and Brad knew he was right about what he said. Brad couldn't do anything but agree with a nod of his head.

He made it back to his office to do some thinking. Should he call Icey or not? His heart wanted him to call her, but his mind told him not to. The last time Brad told Icey something, she used it against him, and all he was trying to do was help her out of love.

Brad quickly made the decision to not say anything else about Pimp to Icey. He would just keep her clear, like Murray said, and focus on building a case on Pimp he could not slick his way out of.

Chapter Eleven

Leave You Out to Dry

Pimp didn't get the messages until he and Icey jumped into the Benz to leave. He saw the many missed calls from Montay and two from his lawyers. Pimp didn't panic at all 'cause he didn't want Icey to witness nothing else. He decided that once they got to the airport, he would call them back.

The message he read about Donte being caught at the condo was what worried him because it was in his name, meaning if Donte don't take the charge, then the feds could charge him.

Pimp would deal with that in a minute, though. He didn't need Icey worried. It was hard enough to get her to say she would leave with him. She didn't know Pimp was plugged in already with the condo and a five-bedroom in Buckhead. He already had shit laid out for them in Atlanta. She just didn't know it yet.

Pimp cranked up the Benz and pulled off. He made Icey leave everything she owned, and he did the same. His cash stash was already at the house, so all he needed to do was make it there. Icey made him promise to let her keep her store and school, and he told her he would. That was the icing on the cake that made her agree to leaving with him.

Atlanta was where Pimp planned to focus and get his father home, raise his child, and marry Icey. She didn't know, but he also was having another store built for her, but in the campcreek area.

They held hands as he drove, headed straight to the airport. Icey was squeezing his hand a little. Pimp smiled, looking over to her. "I love you, baby"

Icey looked over and smiled back. She was happy with the choice she made to come with him. Pimp was not just her man, but he was her child's father, and that meant so, so much to her.

"I love you, too," she replied.

"I know you do. You show you do. That's why I'll do anything for you, it don't matter."

"All I want is for you to behave."

"I promise I'm here, baby. I promise." Pimp spoke from his soul when he made that promise.

It took them thirty minutes to make it to the airport. He had folks already there to help Icey with the small bag she had. Pimp took this time to call Montay, who picked up on the first ring like he was staring at it.

"Hello."

"What's up, bro?" Pimp asked.

"Man, in the air. You know feds got Donte, right?"

"Yeah, just found out 'bout that. I'm 'bout to call my lawyer now, who's been blowing me up all day"

"I thought you was going to the city," Montay said.

"Shit, I am. I should be there in a few hours," replied Pimp, standing outside of the plane.

"Yeah, I'm almost there."

"Bet dat. I'll hit you and keep you posted."

Pimp hung up and called his lawyer, who was already downtown trying to get Donte a bond.

"Savarous, he's in big trouble with this one. You know FBI is about to come at him hard about this one. They will try to get him to slip on you to lessen his sentence, 'cause right now as it stands the government has him by the balls," the lawyer said into the phone.

"So, will you be able to get him a bond?" Pimp

wanted to know so he could process his plan to beat the feds again.

"I don't know. It's worth a try, though. Bad thing about this situation is the condo is leased to your name, and if Donte doesn't take claim for them drugs, then the feds can plant them on you and will plant it on you."

"And what if he didn't, then they charge me. Do you see any way out of it?" Pimp kicked himself for stashing five kilos at the condo. He had forgot to move it.

"Well, yeah, but then you have the money, too. Over a million dollars in cash. They, too, will put these charges on you. You are looking at anywhere from ten to twenty years in the feds, and I know you're not trying to go through that. I know you're not."

His lawyer was right. This was information he needed to know, but didn't want to hear it. He didn't want his plane ride to be thoughts of the federal government finally taking him off the streets.

Pimp hung up with his lawyer 'cause it was time to get on the plane. Icey was waiting on Pimp when he finally got on the G-4 flight to Atlanta. He looked at the woman he loved. He could not let her see the worry he felt. He couldn't show her where he allowed doubt to creep into his thoughts, making him weak and unsure.

Pimp took his seat next to his girl. They took hands, then shared a kiss as the plane vibrated to life. Pimp put his seatbelt on and powered his phone off. Icey did the same.

"Our new life is about to start," said Icey.

"I'm elated to share it with y'all," Pimp shot back. He touched her chin lightly, then her stomach.

Pimp's mind was moving a million miles per hour. He did not let her see it, though. He could not wait 'til they landed in Atlanta so he could push the lawyers to get Donte a bond. Pimp knew he would have to take a trip to North Carolina to get Nevea to go see Donte, make sure he was not running his mouth, thinking Pimp would leave him out dry.

***

Icey was woken up by kisses from Pimp all over her face. She pushed Pimp and opened her eyes. The plane had landed 'cause they weren't moving anymore and Pimp wasn't in his seat anymore.

"Get up, baby," he said and unhooked her seatbelt.

"I'm up, Savarous. Move, bae." Icey was overly tired for some reason, but was glad they made it to Atlanta safe. She hated planes as it was, so any time to get off one, she was happy for that.

Pimp helped her to her feet and led her off the G-4. There was an Escalade awaiting them when they finally stepping off.

Icey was already feeling the safety of being with Pimp by holding hands walking to the SUV. The Atlanta air was calm and cool to her skin. She powered her phone on, and as soon as she did it started ringing. The caller was her mother's number, and Icey decided not to answer because she wasn't ready to answer all the questions her mother had. She knew her mother was worried sick, but Icey knew once they spoke she'd go back to normal. In other words, she would be okay.

Icey sat comfortably in the brand new SUV. Pimp was talking with someone on the phone, and it seemed like a heated conversation. She noticed him hang up, then stuff the phone roughly in his pocket. Pimp had fixed his face by the time he got into the SUV next to her.

Icey just hoped Pimp wasn't about to bring Miami with him to Atlanta 'cause she really couldn't deal with it right then. She needed this thug gangsta stuff to stop.

Without saying a word, she reached out and took his hand. She did it because she wanted him to know she was feeling his frustration. She was there with him through this ordeal.

Pimp gave her small hand a firm squeeze saying he understood her gesture.

Moments later, the SUV pulled off. Pimp's free hand found her stomach. It was the only thing that made him smile as he rubbed it. The feeling was great to Icey. She was in love with the attention she was getting from him.

Her phone rang again, and it was her mother. She sent her to voicemail.

"Why you ducking your mom?" Pimp wanted to know.

Icey blushed her embarrassment for being put on Front Street. "She just worried, that's all."

"So pick up and tell her what's going on," Pimp pressed.

"I got this, bae. I know my mother," Icey said. She patted his chest, still smiling.

"I know you do, baby. I'm just saying I don't want your mom thinking I'm some bad person that got her daughter leaving the state."

"But you are." Icey smiled when she said it.

Pimp laughed a little, then leaned over he gave her a kiss on the jaw before he said, "I'm that good guy you love"

"You're right, baby," replied Icey. "You are so right"

The first place Pimp had them going to was their five-bedroom house in Buckhead in a very nice, classy area. When people rode through this area, they knew there was some money out there. They could tell by the big homes and expensive cars.

When Icey laid her eyes on the bleached, off-white brick and stone house with it's deep green grass, she fell in love with what she saw. Pimp hoped she would like it, but he didn't know, and she didn't give off a sign. All she did was look at the three-car garage with cars already in it.

The Escalade pulled onto the stone driveway. Pimp got out and came around to Icey's side to get the door, not giving the driver a chance to do it. "Come on, baby, let me show you our new home."

He helped Icey out of the SUV. She got a better look, at the same time worried it was drug money or murder money that got him this place. She was worried because they was running from Miami, but the feds were on his trail, so they would soon find them in Atlanta. Icey just wondered how Pimp would explain the house and cars.

Through all her worries, she still managed a smile as Pimp led her up the walkway to their new home.

***

It was home sweet home for Montay. He was more than happy to be home. There wasn't nothing like being on familiar grounds, around real friends, real family, people he knew had his back at all cost. He had been home almost five hours, but this was the first time he'd seen his nine-bedroom mini-mansion since being in Miami.

Montay liked what he saw as he got out of his car: his

fleet of cars all set up, looking good on rims. His wife's cars were also out, parked as expected.

His phone vibrated a message from Pimp saying he made it to the city. Montay text back the okay and pocketed his phone as he entered his home.

He had a small family of three kids and a wife with one dog who lived on the inside of the house and two cooks 'cause his wife Tiffany didn't know how to cook, but it didn't matter to him. Montay had twin boys, seven years old, who he shared with Tiffany and a daughter who was fifteen years old.

Amia was in the chill room with two of her friends when she saw her father. It'd been weeks since they last saw each other, so Amia's face lit up.

"Hey, Daddy!" She jumped up dropping her iPhone between her two best friends. Amia was always daddy's little girl, so she ran into his embrace, missing her father.

"Hey, babydoll." Montay kissed the top of his baby's head. Then he waved to her two friends, some young girls who'd been around them since they were two or three years of age. "Where are your mom and brothers?" he asked.

"Ma's upstairs. Jay and Pacman's in the game room. How are you, dad? I missed you," she hugged him again.

"I missed you, too, babydoll."

Montay made his way into the next room over, which was his man cave, but his twin boys took it over, marking it their game room. With Montay being gone all the time, he didn't put up no fight. Both his son were playing a videogame when he entered their game room.

Jay, the oldest twin, paused the game.

"Daddy!" Pacman, his other twin, jumped up, happy their father was in the house. Montay silently thanked

God for allowing him to make it home to his family 'cause he was feeling their love.

As he was bending down to embrace his boys Tiffany walked in behind him, followed by the dog. Montay didn't notice his wife until he stood to his feet.

"Baby!" Tiffany said.

Montay turned around at the sound of her sexy voice. "The love of my life!"

Tiffany rushed into his arms, missing him just as much as the kids. Hands down, Montay was a good father and outstanding husband. He handled his business as a man, and at the same time he took good care of his friends and the people who helped him get money.

He and Tiffany shared a kiss. He gripped her booty firmly as he tongued her down. Her ass was phat, one of his favorite things about her.

"I'm so glad you're home, baby."

"Me, too," Jay added, then went to grab the joystick to the game he was playing.

They both smiled at their child and walked to their room. He locked in on her phat booty bouncing with each step taken to the room. Montay was realizing he'd missed so much of her the few weeks he's been away.

"We need to talk, too." She looked over her shoulder. Tiffany was such a sexy lady to him, and she knew the affect she had on him, at how he looked at her through a lustful stare.

"Cool," was all Montay said with thoughts of smashing his wife right then and there.

Not only was Tiffany his wife, she was also his business partner. They owned a jewelry store downtown, plus she owned two nail salons. He had a smart wife. She handled all their money issues. She was the one who did the thinking while he went and got the paper. He took the chances to make it happen and she made sure everything was beautiful when it came to their funds.

The inside of their bedroom was like a small apartment. They both had their own walk-in closet, a side room, and 1 ½ baths. Montay found the plushness of his king size bed and fell into it like it was the first time he'd ever seen it, which made his wife laugh at his gesture.

"Best believe that side of the bed miss you, too," Tiffany said.

Montay started playing on his phone as she pulled paperwork out to show him. She climbed up on the bed. "We got the approval. Now we just need to show a steady flow of income." She tossed a stack of papers on his chest.

Montay put the phone to the side and took the papers. When he read them, he was surprised and happy the city allowed him to open up a small casino downtown, which had always been a dream of his.

"So, give or take the next six months, we can create the right amount of paperwork for them to 'yes' us," said Montay and pulled his wife closer to him.

"That's right, baby." She kissed him with a smile.

"Cool."

Even though Montay was one of the biggest drug pushers in Atlanta, he was more legit than dirty. He was a thirty-one year old street nigga who had his time shared in the traps and the trenches. He was a killa stemmed from the gangsta he saw in his father, but he wasn't wild anymore like a teen.

Tiffany also made sure she let him know selling drugs had to stop one day before it got too late. And lately that was all that had been on Montay's mind. Since hooking up with Pimp, Montay had been deep in the streets, running head-on to stuff he was supposed to be running from. He was supposed to be retiring from the game because he'd had success in it and a lucky streak missing a jail cell.

He and his wife shared one more kiss and both got out of the bed. Like always, when Montay was gone and made it back to the house, the whole family would go out somewhere special.

Chapter Twelve

Just Do Not Lie to Me

After a comfortable move in and quick dinner, Pimp left Icey at the house to get stuff in order. He told her he had to meet his lawyer, but really he had to set another plan into action. It was a fact Pimp was worried about Donte folding on him. He called Nevea while jumping into his Benz.

"Hello?"

"Baby girl, 'sup witcha?" It'd been a minute since they last spoke to each other.

"Wassup? Been waiting on you to call. I got a message for you," she said.

He was surprised she remembered his voice. Pimp also knew not to do much talking over the phone, so he said, "I'll be to see you. Are you still in the same spot?"

"I am," was her reply.

"Okay, cool. See you soon."

"Alright," and both of them hung up the phone.

Buckhead was a nice area he was glad Montay turned him onto. Buckhead was big on money and low on the bullshit. It offered the best foods and shopping around the Atlanta area. It gave him a sense of wealth when he mixed and mingled throughout Buckhead or deeper.

Pimp pulled up to a Walgreens and parked the Benz. It was dark out, plus his face wasn't known around here, so Pimp jumped right into a black Mustang with black tint. He looked at the time, knowing he was fifteen minutes behind, so he had to move fast.

The Mustang came to life. Pimp pulled off into the streets. Everything he needed was on the passenger seat next to him. He mashed the gas harder, making the Mustang get down the road at high speeds 'cause time wasn't on his side.

It took him another twenty minutes to pull up to Walmart, where he found a parking spot and waited for the right moment. Even though he was an hour late, he was still on time 'cause he wanted to be in position an hour early. Pimp knew that within minutes, he would finally lay eyes on his target.

For the past few weeks Pimp had planned this day, and today had to be that day it went down 'cause this whole situation was holding him up from moving on in life. Never had anything held Pimp worried, but the feds having Donte was something to make him think about failing his next mission.

Just as his mind wandered, he noticed his mark and a girl walking to their car. Pimp smoothly grabbed his gun with its silencer. He quickly got out of the black Mustang and walked in the direction they were coming.

The guy was the first person to notice Pimp and the gun in his hand, but it was too late to react as Pimp lifted his weapon and fired. The first shot hit the guy between his nose and top lip, the bullet exiting his neck. The woman the man had with him couldn't even get a scream out 'cause Pimp dropped her quick with a few shots to her face and neck.

Panic cranked up the parking lot. It had people running for their lives as Pimp smoothly jumped into the Mustang and eased off into a panicked traffic.

Killing two people in broad daylight was just the start of something Pimp had planned. He had the gun on the passenger seat as he dialed a number in his phone.

Montay picked up. "Yo."

"Bro, what's good? We need to meet and talk," Pimp said.

"I'm out with my family, my guy. It will be later on tonight or something before we link."

"Oh, okay, bet. Just hit me when you free," Pimp shot back and mashed the gas in the Mustang, headed to switch the whips out. He needed Montay to get him a connect to a certain funeral home he had his eye on, but since Montay was busy, Pimp went to his other plan. He dialed 411 in his phone and waited for the operator.

***

Brad and his entire team worked all day pulling everything that was anything on Savarous Jones and his father's past. They dug into Pimp's adult records and realized he was clean all around the surface. Every charge ever brought against him had been dismissed or adquitted. All the people who wrote statements on Pimp were not good people who were worth putting on a stand. So this left the team at a slight standstill.

Brad had more work to do. This would prove to be harder than what he had thought. He was inside his office reading over paperworking, mentally battling himself on what steps to take. He had notes written everywhere to remind him of certain things.

His office door swung open and Jimmy walked in. He had a huge smile on his face, folder in hand, looking directly at Brad. For Brad, this was a good sign to see Jimmy happy about something. That usually meant he had good news and had discovered something major in their favor.

"What's with the great big smile?" Brad wanted to

know. He needed to know, or better yet, needed to hear good news right about then.

Jimmy was slightly bigger than his partner and held a little bit more of a sense of humor than Brad. He did a lil' dance and spun around on his toes. He pointed at Brad with both hands. "Got a shooter, a dealer, and a personal friend that's willing to help us take Savarous down," Jimmy said.

"Update me." He had Brad's full attention right then and there. He was sitting upright now, both hands on his desk, looking at his partner.

"This guy has killed for Savarous, kidnapped for him, and dealt drugs for him. He knows personal stuff, stash houses, and secret meeting places on Pimp," Jimmy informed him, which made Brad smile because that was more than good news.

"This sounds good, Jimmy. So, what's his name? Where is he?"

"His name –"

Jimmy's words came to a sudden stop when his door flew open and his boss walked in. "Pack up, Brad. You and your team is going to Atlanta. Savarous is on the move, has relocated." He tossed a folder on Brad's desk and walked out of the office.

Neither Brad nor Jimmy said anything as Brad took and opened the folder. He read the file, giving a new address on Savarous Jones and his best friend, Icey. With a shake of his head, he closed the folder and stood to his feet. He looked at Jimmy and said, "I guess we go pack, and you can tell me on the plane what's up."

"Okay, cool. Let me go get my things together," Jimmy replied and also left the office, leaving Brad to his own thoughts. He hated this move Icey had made, moving with Pimp to Atlanta. She had an entire career down in Miami. How could she just leave it standing? She was a business owner and a teacher. Did she just quit? Did she really just give up and let it go? Icey couldn't be this dick-drunk, this crazy in love with Savarous like she was acting.

Brad finally got some of his things out of the office, then left to go pack. He had to help Icey because right then she was not helping herself.

The meeting lasted a hour going over new details about the case and enlightment on the move Pimp made to Atlanta. During this hour-long meeting, Brad and Jimmy text each other the conversation they both were having before the boss interrupted them.

Brad was shocked to know one of Pimp's shooters was about to be the one to take him down. He was a close friend with Donte and worked for Pimp on more than one occasion. From what Jimmy text him, the kid knew a lot about Pimp and his business. Nobody knew he was locked down with a baby mother who was due any day now.

After the meeting was over, Jimmy and Brad both went their own ways to handle personal business before going to Atlanta. Brad still had open cases down in Dade County that were fresh, and even had Savarous's name on one or two of them. Inside his car, Brad took out his phone. He went to his contacts and looked at Icey's number. His heart told him to call, but his mind told him different. Love wanted him to help her, but sense made him stay at bay. Icey was too stupid in love. He couldn't get to her, nobody could, so Brad would go at who she loved.

One more stop had to be made by Brad before heading out. Just one more loose end.

***

Nevea was standing in the living room when she saw Pimp pull up with a dude she's never met. They both jumped out of a Bentley fresh, walking up the walkway to her door. It was a Tuesday, so her kids weren't home and her boyfriend was thankfully at work.

She had her phone in hand and headed to the door. Nevea was a social network junkie. She snatched her front door open before Pimp could knock or ring the bell. Like always, she looked good to the eye. Pimp looked her sexy body up and down before he stepped in, followed by Montay.

"What's up, baby girl?" Pimp said while looking around the living room, then proceeded to walk around.

"Ain't nobody in here but us," Nevea said to his back.

Montay just stood there, not saying nothing, looking at the sexy lil' female holding her pink-cased iPhone.

Pimp walk back up front where they was and locked eyes with the pretty girl. "Can't be too careful, sorry. But how you doing? The kids?" Pimp asked.

"I'm doing fine and the kids are at school," she replied.

"Good. So, what's up? What do Donte got going on?"

Nevea walked around Pimp and took a seat on the sofa. She looked down at her phone, then back up to Pimp.

"Feds is still all over you. He said it was some bricks in the condo." That statement from her made Pimp look over to Montay. She continued, "He wanted me to tell you someone gave him up, but he's not talking, so handle your business."

"That's all he said? You sure?" Pimp wanted to know.

"Yeah, that's pretty much it. Oh, he told me to check with Peek and see if he laying low," she remembered.

"Peek?" Pimp was baffled.

"Yeah, that's the nigga who be with Donte," Montay told him.

"Oh, the shooter? Yeah, whe' he at? Whe' he stay, Nevea?" Pimp pressed his question while his mind went to other places, like what was going on and his next move.

"I haven't seen him, but he stay 'round the corner. Got a lil' youngin by Moe's daughter," replied Nevea.

"Ms. Moe's daughter got a kid?" Pimp was shocked.

"Honey, yeah."

"Okay, cool. Tell Donte to believe in me. I got him a get-out-free card, just bear me the time," Pimp told her, and she fully agreed.

"So, what now?" Montay ask Pimp after seeing him hug the sexy female. Montay had other stuff to handle, and being in the game wasn't one of the things he wanted to do.

"We gotta see if he good, first, then we back to the house. Donte just reassured me everything was A-1, so I'm good. I'm not worried 'bout shit else, feel me?" said Pimp, his arm thrown over Nevea's shoulder.

"Well, we need to be making a move on it, huh?" Montay was ready to get it over with.

"Yeah, let's dip."

"Pimp, I need to ask you something privately," Nevea cut in, sounding and looking nervous through her smile.

Pimp had peeped her need to say more, but not in front of Montay, a man he had yet to introduce her to. Pimp smiled, then looked at Montay 'cause he knew it was coming. Montay got the picture, leaving Pimp with little words as he excused himself from the room.

"What's going on, baby girl?" Pimp asked Nevea when he was sure Montay was gone.

Nevea stood to her feet. She had a uncertain, fearful look on her face, a look he couldn't just read, an expression he couldn't figure out. She finally looked over to her closet and opened it wide, giving perfect sight to a safe just sitting there. She turned to look over her shoulder. Seeing Pimp standing there, Nevea punched in a code and the safe cracked open. She stepped to the side and pulled it at the same time.

Pimp saw the safe was packed full with money, so much that not a single dollar bill could fit. Pimp was amazed and surprised at the same time, but what blew his mind was when Nevea pointed to a duffle bag full of more cash.

"He told me to make sure you get this. He say you'll know what to do wit' it. I also took out the money he told me to get, but everything else is there," Nevea spoke once Pimp fully turned to her.

"So, that's you there?" He pointed to the duffle bag.

"No, that's money that couldn't fit. I got mines stashed," she replied

Pimp reached into his pocket to pull out his vibrating phone. It was the call he was expecting, but he didn't answer right then. He pushed the phone back into his pocket.

"Okay, that's what's up. I'll hit you later on what to do 'bout that bread. Do you know how much it is?"

"No. He don't either, I don't think," Nevea said as Pimp hugged her once more.

"Bet."

Pimp and Montay left her spot and hit the highway. He pulled out his cell and started texting back and forth.

Montay, on the other hand, drove and bathed in his own thought about what he needed to do and not do. Pimp wanted his help, but in reality Montay wasn't really trying to lend it. He had family and had already beat the odds of a jail cell. He was ready to retire.

Why was he way up there in North Carolina, anyway, when he had made it to Atlanta? This had to be one of the stupidest moves he'd made in his life, and it was all he could think about.

"Bro, follow the GPS," Pimp said and placed it on the dash. Montay looked and saw it was directed to the airport. *We drove up here, so why we going to the airport?* thought Montay, but he said nothing bout it.

Pimp was making plans in his mind while he continued to text two or three different people, setting stuff up, making plans.

"What's up with you and this funeral home shit, bro? I wanted to ask." Montay wanted to know because Pimp wanted him to get him some keys made.

"Oh, I'll put you up on that later. It's beautiful, though." Pimp didn't take his eyes off the phone when he replied to Montay's question.

"You know the senator's daughter and boyfriend was killed. That's the funeral home the daughter is in. You know I'm solid, I just wanna know do you got anything to do with it?" Montay shot another question.

It made Pimp finally look up and smile before saying, "Hell nawl, bro. I'm not the one that did that work." Pimp then laughed.

"You know I'm witcha, shawty. I just wanted to know 'cause I know how crazy you can get and shit," said

Montay, defending his question.

"Nawl, bro. I'm just trying to reach a couple more millions by hustling 'cause killing ain't gonna bring no money," Pimp told him, and Montay felt exactly where he was coming from.

They drove thirty more minutes and finally pulled up to the airport, which was busy and heavy with traffic. People were everywhere, all shapes and sizes, colors and sexes coming and going.

Montay parked the rental and Pimp got out, stepping into the warm, bright day. He looked to the entrance of the airport to see if he could see who he was looking for. Pimp searched every female face he saw, but he still didn't see her.

Right when Pimp pulled out his phone, he heard her voice and smelled her flavor from the blowing air. Pimp turned around when he heard, "You looking for me, mister?"

A smile came to Pimp's face when he saw Honey looking as amazing as he'd ever seen her. She was still sexy as ever. Pimp walked over and gave her a hug.

"What's up, boo?" Pimp asked.

"Hey." She hugged him back, then allowed him to grab her bags. After she and the bags were safe in the backseat, Pimp jumped up front.

"Montay, Honey. Honey, Montay," Pimp introduced them and Montay cranked up to pull off.

"What's up, miss lady?" Montay spoke while moving through the parking lot, searching for an exit.

"Hello," Honey spoke back, then started digging in a bag, looking for something. She found what she was looking for and pulled a picture out, giving it to Pimp. When Pimp looked at the picture, he wasn't surprised to see Brad and his partner. Pimp wondered how Honey managed to get her hands on it.

"How you get this?" questioned Pimp and passed the picture to Montay.

"He came to my job. He asked questions about you, us, and the team. You know I played dumbfounded all the way to a T," Honey replied.

Pimp turned, looked at her, and winked. She winked back, and that's when he saw blackness around her eye. Pimp reached back and grabbed her face. He turned it a lil' and knew he was right. Her eye was black.

"Who did this?" Pimp asked.

"It's noth–"

"I said who, not what it was!"

"Rodney."

"Yo' boyfriend?"

"My ex. I left his ass," she shot back.

"And where is your daughter?"

"With my auntie. I'm going to get her when I get settled in. I just couldn't stay around him anymore, point blank."

Pimp said nothing else during the ride on the highway. Like always, his mind was moving a million miles per hour, trying to figure out a plan.

Montay drove while Pimp thought deep and Honey slept. Something had to give with this dude Brad and all this police shit. Pimp knew his hand was being forced and his back was being placed against the wall. Life was about to take a sudden turn for someone.

***

Brad wasn't surprised when he got to Icey and Pimp's

home and saw it was nice. Jimmy sat in the passenger seat going over a file while Brad just watched the new home. The only movement had been from the workers, with no sign of Pimp or Icey since they got there. Brad had read all the files on Pimp and Atlanta. The only case they could get on him was tax evasion, which was nothing. They would have to build a case on Pimp and all his friends until they had enough to drop the cuffs around his wrists.

Brad started recording a video of the home and the cars parked. They took down every plate on each car, then Jimmy made notes.

Brad knew Icey was the only person home other than the help, and the last thing he wanted to do was be seen by her, so he pulled off after cranking.

Brad had determination in his mind and in his heart. He was determined to figure out Pimp's every move down to the most detailed gesture. He was so ready to see the look on Icey's face when Pimp finally went down. It would be joy to his soul. It would be a hard day for Icey, but every tear would be worth the cry, and in the end she would love Brad for having her best interests at heart.

"One thing about it, two things for certain," Jimmy said out of nowhere.

"What?" asked Brad.

"Pimp is a made man. He jumped from city to city, pretty girl to pretty girl. You gotta have it made, living like that."

"See, if his ass have it made in a federal cell for the next fifty years, I bet he can't show me made then," Brad said and meant what he said.

"I know, right?"

"But anyway, explain to me this witness."

"Oh yeah, this guy is a key puzzle piece in this case. He was a shooter for Pimp who has shot and also killed people for Pimp. He has solid information that matches up to paperwork we have. He has pictures, text messages, and even video of some events."

"Wow."

"Yeah. He was caught in Miami a few hours before Donte was caught. We got two tips where both guys was and snatched them both up."

"So, we are looking good so far. I'm loving this update. Once we get settled in, we will bring the team up on everything we have," Brad said to his partner.

"And if we can get Donte to talk, Lord," Jimmy added.

Brad agreed with a shake of his head and an offer to fist pound. At the same time they knew Donte would be hard-pressed. Really, they didn't need Donte to convict nobody, but he could be key if he flipped.

"We gotta get statements from those teenagers on the home invasion case, as well, because they know a whole lot of stuff. Shit they haven't even said yet," Brad said as his mind wandered.

Jimmy, on the other hand, had pulled up a picture of Montay. "His face has been seen a lot lately."

Brad looked over, then said, "That's nobody." He then reached over and changed the photo to a picture of Pimp. "He's our main target. Him!"

"I can clearly see you have the hots for this guy," Jimmy replied through a laugh.

"My best friend is in the middle of this. You know I can taste this man's blood," Brad quickly admitted.

"And I finally understand your drive. And I'm here to help you, my friend, 'cause I love Icey, too."

"Now, that's what I wanna hear." They pounded each other again.

Brad made it to the downtown Atlanta headquarters. The day had just gotten started for both men. They hadn't even had the chance to unpack or anything because they went from the airport to Icey's house. Brad pulled into the parking garage and killed the engine. He was feeling good about his chances with this case now. All he had to do was put everything in its right place, leaving Pimp's lawyers no loophole to escape. This meant he must be near perfect with ever move he made.

***

Back in Atlanta, Pimp had it confirmed that the informant was Donte's shooter, the young killa Pimp took a liking to. It wasn't a surprise that even a killa folded, but it was a blow to his plan and an obstacle to his mission. Pimp took Honey to his condo and he and Montay rode to Montay's crib.

"So, what do you think?" Pimp asked, breaking the silence that captured the car.

Montay's mind was somewhere else, so he didn't catch the question. "Huh?"

"What you think about this informant? What you think them folks got cooking?" Pimp just wanted to see where Montay's head was, where his thoughts was, because he had his own.

Montay finally caught on to what Pimp was saying, then responded, "Shid, that we need to see it. That this nigga don't shed light on our darkness because if he do, then it's gonna be a cold day in hell," Montay told Pimp and was as serious as a heart attack.

"Don't you got contacts and shit in Rice Street?" asked Pimp.

"Yeah, I can hit da mob. You know them boys run the street." Montay told Pimp about Goodfellas, a new Atlanta gang to most folks, but just a gang that's been frontline since day one to those who really knew.

"Well, yeah, you need to silence him ASAP," Pimp said quickly as he got a reply from Montay.

"I'm on it." Montay started going through his phone contacts, looking for a certain number to get straight to business.

Pimp wanted this gunner dead before nightfall and everything would be okay. He could continue to execute his plan, his movement, because it was near.

Montay got someone on the phone and spoke. He quickly lined the hit up with someone on the other end of the phone as Pimp drove.

After dropping Montay back at his ride, Pimp made his way home to the house. He was ready to see his love, his wifey, his baby-ma-to-be.

Tomorrow would mark another day with a list of things to get out of the way. The game was getting cold, shit was getting real, and Pimp was getting prepared for the let-down.

Alone inside the whip, Pimp tuned in on the radio. He cut it up and rode the highway to Buckhead.

Jerry Jackson

Chapter Thirteen

That's Why I Fucks with You

Icey was so happy when she finally laid eyes on her man. She had been missing him all day like crazy on top of being scared, worried that something may happen. Pimp had made it home safe, and she thanked God for it.

When he walked into the room, she was sitting up in the bed. He closed the door, not taking his eyes off her. His lustful stare and cute features captivated her. Being pregnant also granted her mixed emotions.

Pimp leaned down toward her and she wrapped her arms around the one she loved.

"'Sup, baby? How y'all doing?" Pimp asked, giving her a quick kiss and awaiting a reply.

Icey smiled 'cause she missed her man dearly. "We are just fine, and also grateful you're home and safe," she shot back, touching his baby-face. Icey was hoping their child looked just like him, either boy or girl, it don't even matter.

"You done unpacking some of your things, baby? You like this room, right?" Pimp lay next to her on the bed. he sent Montay a quick text, then read a message from Honey.

"I love this room. I'm not done unpacking; however, I have the entire weekend to handle my business on that. But this house, I think, is too big, baby," Icey replied.

"Of course not. Not with having three of my kids," Pimp said with a smile.

"Honey boo."

"So, yo' boy Brad is going at me hard. Don't be surprised if you don't see him lurking around the corner."

"Brad better sit down. I think he got enough heat under him as it is," she quickly shot back. Icey lay down beside him. She tossed one leg over him, nestled under him, her head on his chest.

"Well, he all in other states trying to get folks to flip me. He crazy, baby. I'm not understanding your boy, but hey," was all Pimp could say.

Icey didn't say anything at all because no matter what anyone thought, no matter what they could or would say, she was in love with Pimp, and that was how she planned to remain.

Atlanta was their new home. She was pregnant and happy about it. She was content with her entire situation, and Brad needed to stay out of her business. She was beginning to hate his guts. She was so hateful toward just the thought of him that she wanted to text him, but at the same time she prayed he would just forget them. Icey didn't believe in her heart that Brad was pressed on Pimp. She just couldn't believe it.

Pimp was texting back and forth on his phone. Icey was just glad he was home and not in the streets. She didn't say another word. She was content in their place right then.

Pimp, on the other hand, got the confirmation he wanted from Montay. Everything was set and ready to go. Even the gunner whould get what was coming to him was the message from Montay. There was a price with it, but there also was a reward, so Pimp had not one problem paying the ticket.

He text Honey also, telling her he'd see her in the morning, on time as planned, and told her not to be late.

After that, Pimp placed his phone on the side of him opposite of his love, his life, his baby-mother-to-be. Pimp turned toward her. He pulled her closer, feeling her warmth and readiness. He felt the heat between her thighs as one of her legs was tossed over his own.

They shared a deep kiss. Icey gave him some candy-flavored tongue, then Pimp sucked her bottom lip, pulling her even closer. Her pussy pressed to his thigh. She kinda rolled her hips, arching her back as one of his hands gripped her booty. They kissed some more as Icey's hand slid down his stomach. She pulled his shirt up, then slid her hands down his pants without warning.

"Mm," said Pimp as she held his growing member in her palms, stroking him to a hardened brick. Pimp turned Icey completely on her back and rose up to look down at the beauty she held. He kissed her nose lightly, then her lips. His hand slid between her legs and she opened them as wide as she could get them as he rubbed her softly, but firmly. Icey was moist. Pimp pulled her panties to the side and, with one finger, he moved it up and down between her pussy lips. She was wet, and Pimp was really, really hard.

They kissed deep some more as Pimp started slowly finger-fucking her wetness. Icey rolled her hips onto his finger and it felt great. she had her eyes closed and her hopes high.

Pimp removed his finger dripping with her juices. He positioned himself between her legs and held his dick at the base. He rubbed his head over and around her pussy, coating his dick with her warm juices.

"I love you," Icey moaned as Pimp slid up inside her walls. She was tight, but welcoming.

"I love you," Pimp added and started stroking his girl deep, feeling her tense and relax as his pace quickened. They kissed, he stroked, she rolled and accepted the love he was giving. Pimp realized at that moment he had been missing his girl a lot. He realized that no other female mattered to him like Icey did.

Pimp put one of her ankles beside his neck. He turned his face and kissed the side of her feet while he continued to thrust inside of her. Icey moaned her reply to his lovemaking. Pimp got in a push-up position and started beating her walls up.

"Yes, just li-like that, baby!" said Icey as she held onto him. Pimp kept at his pace. He ground and thrust into her as they kissed and sucked on each other.

After Icey finally reached her valley, Pimp shot his load deep into her tunnel of love. They both found sleep shortly after rolling into a cuddling position, Pimp's mind on love and murder and Icey's mind on the future.

**

"Daddy! Daddy! Mommy said get up! Get up, Daddy!" Montay's youngest child said. Montay was balled up in the soft comfort of his king size bed. When he opened his eyes, the master bedroom was filled with bright sunlight. He couldn't do anything but smile and drop his face back into the pillow.

"Tell yo' ma I'll be down there," Montay said into the pillow. He was still feeling the affects of being tired from last night. He looked up at the clock and got even more tired when he saw the time was 9:30. His son left the room to do as told. He rolled over onto his back and for a moment just stared at the ceiling, lost in thought.

Montay reached over and grabbed his phone. He read a text from Pimp and another text confirming the hit had gone down as planned.

As soon as he was about to get out of bed, his wife walked into the room. She had an apron wrapped around her. Knowing she was cooking breakfast had him hungry.

"Yo' brothers are downstairs," she said, and Montay instantly sat up because when she said brothers, it only meant one thing because Montay was the only child to his mom and dad.

"Downstairs?" he began to get out of the bed. "How many?"

"Three, Meco among them," his wife replied.

Montay quickly got right, washed his face, brushed his teeth, then headed downstairs, already knowing what was up.

When he made it to his living room, Meco and two of his top gunners sat quietly. Meco was one of the head GF members who had a lock on Atlanta. Anything that went down in the city had to come through his crew.

"What's up, bruh?" Montay said once he joined them.

Meco just looked at him a moment, then he spoke. "You paid a pretty penny for that face. One of my brothers handled that and got t' walk with that body 'cause he got caught red-handed. My folks wanna know why. And who is this nigga Pimp?" Meco asked and Montay didn't waste no time explaining the situation.

"Okay, the nigga was working with the feds. He had me and Pimp by the balls if we didn't ice him. Pimp is a nigga from North Carolina. We met years ago doing business."

"So, you known him years?" Meco cut in with a question.

"Yeah, 'bout six years. This the nigga I got that jewelry from. He found a spot in Miami that was pumping, asked me to link, and that's how shit happened," Montay told him.

"Well, the wolf jumped down on me to see what was what. His message to you is, per the wolf, we run Atlanta. Nothing is bigger than us. If your man's not approved to play in the city, then he's off. Make sure he watch his step 'cause it's plenty toes in the streets," Meco said and got a nod of the head from Montay 'cause he understood loud and clear.

Montay knew Atlanta was different. Atlanta was run by Gangsta and Kash, two true legends of the city, and they did not play no game. They had structured. They had everything working together. Every gang, every crew was eating, and the police wasn't in their mix.

He knew Pimp would have to tread light through Atlanta or Gangsta would have him removed in the worst way. Montay completely understood and made the decision to quickly tell Pimp what was going on.

Meco kicked it over a few more, then Montay walked him and his gunners to the car. "Make sure you holla at ya boy." Meco jumped into the Benz.

"I gotcha. Two luv, bru."

"Twice." Meco closed the door and the Benz pulled off.

Montay made his way back into the house. He closed his door, then reached for his phone. He would go ahead and put Pimp on point about Gangsta and the Wolf.

When he dialed Pimp's number, the phone just rang until his voicemail picked up. Montay then sent him a text message telling him to call.

His wife was making up the bed when he walked back into their bedroom. "Everything okay, baby?" she asked.

"Yeah, bae. Everything is good," Montay said as he made his way over to his wife. He pulled her into his embrace for a kiss. "Love you."

"And I love you," was her reply, and another kiss.

***

She pulled up to the funeral home on time, as planned. When Honey parked in the spot, she noticed Pimp sitting inside a white van, as expected. Honey kinda blushed, but quickly fixed her face because she had something to do.

Honey was back up to her no-good ways again. She was back in the streets and back with Pimp. This time she wouldn't go out bad and allow Pimp to get away if she helped him out of this slump he was in.

Honey knew the day she saw Pimp at the gas station that she was still down for him, that she still loved him and wanted to be with him. She tried to move on with Rodney. She tried to live her life without Pimp in it, but as soon as she saw him, as soon as she saw he needed her help, she was there, no matter what. No matter how anyone felt, her love for Pimp was far greater than she expected it to be.

Rodney's insecure actions didn't help the situation at all. He made matters worse by always bringing Pimp's name up in every conversation they had. It got to the point that all Honey could do was think about Pimp all the time, non-stop, and when the feds came to her job about Pimp, she knew they were meant to be together. She knew she was his angel and she was ready to play her position.

Honey got out of the Benz in her best jeans and heels. She knew she had it going on and almost always stopped traffic where she was seen. She felt Pimp's eyes all over her body, making her nervous. More nervous than she'd ever been.

Inside the funeral home, she was met at the front desk by an old white man. The funeral home smelled like fresh flowers and dry blood, a mixture she didn't like, but she dealt with it because she had a plan to execute.

"Hello, how are you doing? I am trying to get the directions on a service for my father," Honey said to the man who looked at her with a lustful stare. She watched his eyes travel from her face to her breast, supported by a push-up bra. Honey leaned her weight on one leg, making her hip poke out. She gave her sexy stare. The old white man couldn't help but be captivated by what he saw. He licked his lips before he spoke.

"Okay, there's proper paperwork you must fill out."

"Okay, let's get the process done," Honey said.

Meanwhile, Pimp had crept inside the funeral home through the basement. He was dressed in all black with a backpack on and baseball cap. He made sure to wear gloves 'cause this investigation was about to get deep.

Pimp made his way through the basement where dead bodies awaited attention. He saw neither the girl nor the dude he killed, but knew they were there. He continued to look and make his way up the steps.

This was the part where he knew he had to be careful and not be seen by either visitors or the owner. Pimp crept slowly up the steps and listened hard until he heard Honey's voice talking up front, as planned. This gave him a bit of comfort, but he was still on point moving to the top of the steps.

Pimp stopped when he reached the last step. He peeked around the corner left and right, looking down the hallway that was painted oak red. Pictures were hung up and flower pots lined the walls. There were rooms on each side of the hallway. Pimp quickly dashed into one, which had to be the wrong one because it had an old white man in the casket. Pimp looked across the hall into another room, but that wasn't the one he was looking for, either.

He heard Honey continue to talk. Pimp walked into another room and hit jackpot. He took off his bookbag, moving fast. He unzipped it while on the floor.

He pulled out a bomb and tool box. It was time to get to work.

***

Meco pulled up, driven by his driver. He and his top gunners got out of the Benz and were escorted into a gated area, restricted only for a helicopter. Once in the helicopter, Meco and his men had to give up the weapons they carried.

The fly over was only two minutes. Meco has been there a few times, so he knew the rules. The home they landed at was the biggest house Meco has ever laid his eyes on. It was at least a twenty-bedroom pad with fields of glass on all sides, pools, a basketball court, baseball and tennis areas. Meco saw over ten exotic whips, a few Benz and Bentleys, and a couple regular cars.

The three GF members were led from the chopper to a walkway, then to two golf carts that would take them to the big homie's house. Meco was one of the riches GF member out of Atlanta, and the thanks goes to two people: Da Wolf and Big Homie. These were some dudes Meco met in prison and linked up with, and everyone stayed solid and loyal. Everyone handled good business that continued from the cells to the condos.

Even though Meco was a good fella and Da Wolf and

Big Homie wasn't, his loyalty was still with them just as much as it was with the mob. Meco would never cross the mob, but he'd never cross his two partners, his life line, his connect.

Meco and his gunners walked into the spacious home and were greeted by the great smell of food. Every time Meco came out, he always felt like he was home, in his comfort zone.

They were met by a servant who they followed into the den area. Inside the den, posted around a pool table, were Kash and Gangsta. Meco walked over to both his partners, leaving his gunners standing in the middle of the floor. He embraced first Kash, then Gangsta.

"What's going on?" Kash was first to speak.

"Da mob," Meco shot back as always, then he gave dap to Gangsta.

"'Sup, foo'?" Gangsta added. Gangsta and Kash were two dudes Meco met in prison, and they'd become some powerful men. They had more than a city on lock. They had states fucked up.

Meco had been in with them the past five years and had become very, very rich under the command of both friends. It was love then, and it was love now.

"So, have a seat. Tell ya boys to fall back." Kash looked to the gunners. Meco told them to relax and get comfortable. One of Gangsta's servants escorted both gunners out of the room into an entertainment room.

Gangsta and Kash also took seats where Meco was. Gangsta needed some understanding about this new dude Meco brought to the city. Gangsta didn't waste no time getting straight to the point.

"What's up with this nigga you told Kash 'bout?"

"Oh, the lil nigga officially stamp from Montay. He

'bout his issue and his check, right."

"Why he not staying in Miami?" Gangsta asked.

Meco thought for a moment before he spoke. He didn't want to say the wrong thing. He didn't want to make Montay's word look bad. "Shawty crunk up a trap in Dade. Shit was booming so hard that them niggas started hating. Bruh, he a killa, so he shot most the pockets off them suckas. Police got involved. Feds came into the picture, so bruh fell back," Meco explained.

"So, what's his plans in the city?" Gangsta cut in with his question.

"To tell you the truth, I'on know, but I was thinking we bring him into the team. Y'all niggas will like him," Meco added.

He knew his words alone would connect Pimp, but now he needed Pimp to see the big picture and listen. See, Pimp was the solo-type guy. He was his own leader and took orders from no man. But with Kash and Gangsta, it was another level. With them it was about the chain of command. They had a operation going that made everyone rich. Every gang, every hood, every trap was doing what it do under the orders of Da Wolf.

Meco knew Gangsta had enough to help Pimp out of the fed case. All he had to do was get him in good with the team.

"Well, first thing first, all that hot shit, that murder shit, we not 'bout to have at all. Murder rate is down 6%. We changing our city for the good. Another thing: no drug shipments. All drug trade money fold come through us. He must know this and comply," Kash told Meco, and Gangsta nodded his agreement.

Meco could work with that. He wanted to set up a date where they could meet Pimp. He knew either Kash or

Gangsta already had their intel on Pimp and knew everything there was to know about him.

"Just make sure he keep it low in our city. We the ones who makes the noise here," Gangsta spoke also.

"Will do," Meco replied.

"So, this nigga Pimp. He got hustle? You think he can hold a whole state down?" asked Kash.

"No doubt. No doubt at all," Meco shot back.

Kash and Gangsta both started laughing.

**

Brad and Jimmy both had to play escort for the funeral of the senator's daughter and boyfriend. Their boss was good friends with the senator, ex-judge, ex-attorney general. It was a sad day, and the senator was taking the death of his daughter very, very hard.

His entire family was there, and all of his true friends and the love was still not enough. The warmth couldn't replace his only child, his daughter, a very beautiful, bright woman. No amount of love could replace her life.

For Brad it was just a typical day. A sad day, but just a day for him to make an earning. The funeral would last no more than three hours. He had office work today. He and Jimmy needed to put the paperwork together they obtained over the past two weeks. They needed to interview suspects and witnesses.

Brad wasn't trying to slip no kind of way, slack in no kind of fashion 'cause any little thing could mess the entire case up and Pimp would get away clean, and that alone would kill Brad's hopes and dreams.

The funeral was jam-packed. Family and friends filled the streets with many different cars. The Secret Service,

FBI, and the local cops also were deep out. Jimmy was the driver while Brad sat shotgun. Their boss and his wife was seated comfortable in the backseat.

There were judges, lawyers, the D.A. and all kinds of figures attending the funeral. It was one of the biggest funerals Brad had ever witnessed.

All the cars and vans lined up and headed toward the church where the service was being held. Not one time did Brad or Jimmy try to figure out what happened to the senator's daughter. All Brad knew was she was murdered in cold blood in broad daylight. This was someone else's case. It wasn't Brad's business at all unless the government saw fit for him to get on the case. Savarous Jones's case was much greater than a double homicide, Brad thought.

After an hour of driving car-behind-car, they finally made it to the church. Friends and family were already there, along with bystanders and everyone else and their mother. The church was packed. There was literally nowhere to park. Police had to block off both ends of the street in order for the family to park. They all parked in the middle of the road.

Brad followed everyone else's lead and killed the motor. He and Jimmy got out of the car first to scan the streets as they were trained to do. Then, with one swift motion, both back doors opened, allowing both husband and wife to be escorted inside the church behind a grieving family.

The church settings were beautifully placed. It was a sad, but outstanding moment. An all-white funeral, pink light roses, and yellow ribbons were the church's attire as everyone wore white. Brad and Jimmy escorted their boss and his wife to their seats. After that, Jimmy and Brad walked to the back of the church to watch from a distance.

***

Pimp waited another twenty minutes until the preacher started preaching. He was inside the van listening to the preacher from a mic he plated on one of the caskets. He waited three blocks down and finally crunk up the van to get ready to leave.

Pimp had in his lap a remote. It had two green buttons on it. If Pimp pressed either button, the bomb would explode.

Pimp mashed them both and instantly heard the bomb go off from three blocks down. At the same time, he was pulling into traffic.

From there on out everything should fall into place. It should be a cake walk for his father to get out of prison. The right judge got killed, and at least a dozen more. Some federal agents were killed and the government attorney general. Pimp didn't care if he made a sad day a sadder moment. All he wanted was his father out of prison.

Pimp would chill now. He could retire out of the game, go legit one time, and be good. His girl was happy and he was happy.

Thirty minutes into the drive, he switched from the van to a rental truck. Pimp was a rich man now with another chance, a fresh start in a brand new city, a beautiful city with life moving at a fast pace.

Honey was in place at the hotel when he got there. Pimp saw she had all the money from Donte in stacks on one of the beds. She had a glock laying next to her with music playing out of her phone. Her loyalty was what

Pimp loved about her. She was so down for him, always there, always had his back.

Honey smiled when he walked in, glad to see him safe. "Hey, daddy."

"'Sup? How much?"

"Baby, I haven't even counted it yet. I'm waiting on the three money machines to get here," she replied as Pimp sat on the other bed, pulling his phone out.

He found the remote and clicked on the news, and it was breaking news. *Bomb Explodes at Funeral* was the headline. Under it was printed *66 Dead So Far.*

"Look! Look!" Pimp told Honey, who was equally shocked to see the Federal agents in the midst. It wasn't in the plan to kill them, but Pimp was glad it happened like it did 'cause Brad was on his ass.

Pimp picked his phone up. He opened it to see he had a text from Montay: *We need to meet.*

When? What time? Pimp sent one back and wondered what it was about.

He sat around the next couple hours with Honey and counted the money. There was two million in cash. Pimp was proud to know his lil' homie was holding his part down.

"So, what's the next move, baby?" Honey asked. She was kinda exhausted from the two-hour-long money count. She was laid back on the bed looking at Pimp, who was replying to a text message.

"Shid, I'ma set you up straight. I was thinking starting a record lable or something. Open some clothing store or some shit, and I need the team. I'm really done with this street shit," Pimp said over his shoulder.

Honey missed him. She was still drove over this man, point-blank, period. Pimp pocketed his phone, then stood up. He finally was ready to just sit back, let his dad taste freedom, raise his kid, and marry Icey.

"I'm with whatever you're with, boo. You know this," Honey added and stood up, also.

"Listen, I need you to know I got a lil one on the way. I also have a relationship going with the mother, as well, but that don't dictate how we rock. It don't change my love for you," Pimp told Honey. He said it 'cause he felt like she could handle the truth. And he was right.

"I'm with you, Pimp. Whatever, however it go," Honey confirmed.

Pimp liked what he heard. It kinda felt funny 'cause he held a lil doubt that she wasn't gonna like this news.

Pimp pulled her into his arms. He lifted her face up toward his own.

"That's why I fucks with you, babygirl. I swear"

To Be Continued
The Heart of a Gangsta 3
Coming Soon

Stay Connected with Us!

Text **LOCKDOWN** to 22828 to stay up-to-date with new releases, sneak peaks, contests and more…

Thank you!

Jerry Jackson

BOW DOWN TO MY GANGSTA

By **Ca$h & Jamaica**

TORN BETWEEN TWO

By **Coffee**

BLOOD OF A BOSS **IV**

By **Askari**

BRIDE OF A HUSTLA **III**

By **Destiny Skai**

WHEN A GOOD GIRL GOES BAD **II**

By **Adrienne**

LOVE & CHASIN' PAPER **II**

By **Qay Crockett**

THE HEART OF A GANGSTA **III**

By **Jerry Jackson**

LOYAL TO THE GAME **IV**

By **T.J. & Jelissa**

A DOPEBOY'S PRAYER **II**

By **Eddie "Wolf" Lee**

TRUE SAVAGE **III**

By **Chris Green**

IF LOVING YOU IS WRONG... **II**

By **Jelissa**

BLOODY COMMAS **III**

The Heart of a Gangsta 2

By **T.J. Edwards**
BLAST FOR ME **II**
By **Ghost**
A DISTINGUISHED THUG STOLE MY HEART **II**
By **Meesha**
ADDICTIED TO THE DRAMA **II**
By **Jamila Mathis**

Available Now

RESTRAINING ORDER **I & II**
By **CA$H & Coffee**
LOVE KNOWS NO BOUNDARIES **I II & III**
By **Coffee**
RAISED AS A GOON I, II & III
By **Ghost**
LAY IT DOWN **I & II**
LAST OF A DYING BREED
By **Jamaica**
LOYAL TO THE GAME
LOYAL TO THE GAME II
LOYAL TO THE GAME III
By **TJ & Jelissa**
BLOODY COMMAS

Jerry Jackson

By **T.J. Edwards**
IF LOVING HIM IS WRONG…
By **Jelissa**
A DISTINGUISHED THUG STOLE MY HEART
By **Meesha**
PUSH IT TO THE LIMIT
By **Bre' Hayes**
BLOOD OF A BOSS **I II & III**
By **Askari**
THE STREETS BLEED MURDER **I, II & III**
THE HEART OF A GANGSTA
By **Jerry Jackson**
CUM FOR ME
CUM FOR ME 2
CUM FOR ME 3
An **LDP Erotica Collaboration**
BRIDE OF A HUSTLA **I & II**
THE FETTI GIRLS **I, II& II**
By **Destiny Skai**
WHEN A GOOD GIRL GOES BAD
By **Adrienne**
A GANGSTER'S REVENGE **I II III & IV**
THE BOSS MAN'S DAUGHTERS
THE BOSS MAN'S DAUGHTERS II

160

A SAVAGE LOVE **I & II**

BAE BELONGS TO ME

A HUSTLER'S DECEIT I, II

By **Aryanna**

A KINGPIN'S AMBITON

A KINGPIN'S AMBITION **II**

I MURDER FOR THE DOUGH

By **Ambitious**

TRUE SAVAGE

TRUE SAVAGE II

By **Chris Green**

A DOPEBOY'S PRAYER

By **Eddie "Wolf" Lee**

WHAT ABOUT US **I & II**

NEVER LOVE AGAIN

THUG ADDICTION

By **Kim Kaye**

THE KING CARTEL **I, II & III**

By **Frank Gresham**

THESE NIGGAS AIN'T LOYAL **I, II & III**

By **Nikki Tee**

GANGSTA SHYT **I II &III**

By **CATO**

THE ULTIMATE BETRAYAL

Jerry Jackson

By **Phoenix**
BOSS'N UP **I & II**
By **Royal Nicole**
I LOVE YOU TO DEATH
By Destiny J
I RIDE FOR MY HITTA
I STILL RIDE FOR MY HITTA
By **Misty Holt**
LOVE & CHASIN' PAPER
By **Qay Crockett**
TO DIE IN VAIN
By **ASAD**

<u>BOOKS BY LDP'S CEO, CA$H</u>

<u>TRUST IN NO MAN</u>

<u>TRUST IN NO MAN 2</u>

<u>TRUST IN NO MAN 3</u>

<u>BONDED BY BLOOD</u>

<u>SHORTY GOT A THUG</u>

<u>THUGS CRY</u>

<u>THUGS CRY 2</u>

<u>THUGS CRY 3</u>

<u>TRUST NO BITCH</u>

<u>TRUST NO BITCH 2</u>

<u>TRUST NO BITCH 3</u>

<u>TIL MY CASKET DROPS</u>

<u>RESTRAINING ORDER</u>

<u>RESTRAINING ORDER 2</u>

<u>IN LOVE WITH A CONVICT</u>

<u>Coming Soon</u>

BONDED BY BLOOD 2

BOW DOWN TO MY GANGSTA

Jerry Jackson

CPSIA information can be obtained
at www.ICGtesting.com
Printed in the USA
LVHW080742110119
603457LV00020BA/780/P

9 781982 001421